TOM CLANCY'S NET FORCE®

*Don't miss any of these exciting adventures
starring the teens of Net Force . . .*

VIRTUAL VANDALS

The Net Force Explorers go head-to-head with a group of
teenage pranksters on-line—and find out firsthand that virtual bullets can kill you!

THE DEADLIEST GAME

The virtual Dominion of Sarxos is the most popular war
game on the Net. But someone is taking the game too seriously . . .

ONE IS THE LONELIEST NUMBER

The Net Force Explorers have exiled Roddy—who sabo-
taged one program too many. But Roddy's created a new
"playroom" to blow them away . . .

THE ULTIMATE ESCAPE

Net Force Explorer pilot Julio Cortez and his family are
being held hostage. And if the proper authorities refuse to
help, it'll be the Net Force Explorers to the rescue!

THE GREAT RACE

A virtual space race against teams from other countries will
be a blast for the Net Force Explorers. But someone will go
to any extreme to sabotage the race—even murder . . .

END GAME

An exclusive resort is suffering Net thefts, and Net Force
Explorer Megan O'Malley is ready to take the thief down.
But the criminal has a plan to put her out of commission—
permanently . . .

(continued . . .)

CYBERSPY

A "wearable computer" permits a mysterious hacker access to a person's most private thoughts. It's up to Net Force Explorer David Gray to convince his friends of the danger—before secrets are revealed to unknown spies . . .

SHADOW OF HONOR

Was Net Force Explorer Andy Moore's deceased father a South African war hero or the perpetrator of a massacre? Andy's search for the truth puts every one of his fellow students at risk . . .

PRIVATE LIVES

The Net Force Explorers must delve into the secrets of their commander's life—to prove him innocent of murder . . .

SAFE HOUSE

To save a prominent scientist and his son, the Net Force Explorers embark on a terrifying virtual hunt for their enemies—before it's too late . . .

GAMEPREY

A gamer's convention turns deadly when virtual reality monsters escape their confines—and start tracking down the Net Force Explorers!

DUEL IDENTITY

A member of a fencing group lures the Net Force Explorers to his historical simulation site—where his dream of ruling a virtual nation is about to come true, but only at the cost of their lives . . .

DEATHWORLD

When suicides are blamed on a punk/rock/morbo Web site, Net Force Explorer Charlie Davis goes onto the site undercover—and unaware of its real danger . . .

HIGH WIRE

The only ring Net Force Explorer Andy Moore finds in a virtual circus is a black market ring—in high-tech weapons software and hardware . . .

TOM CLANCY'S
NET FORCE®

COLD CASE

CREATED BY

Tom Clancy and **Steve Pieczenik**

Written by
Bill McCay

BERKLEY JAM BOOKS, NEW YORK

If you purchased this book without a cover, you should be aware that
this book is stolen property. It was reported as "unsold and destroyed"
to the publisher, and neither the author nor the publisher has received
any payment for this "stripped book."

This is a work of fiction. Names, characters, places, and incidents are
either the product of the author's imagination or are used fictitiously,
and any resemblance to actual persons, living or dead, business
establishments, events, or locales is entirely coincidental.

TOM CLANCY'S NET FORCE: COLD CASE

A Berkley Jam Book / published by arrangement with
Netco Partners

PRINTING HISTORY
Berkley Jam edition / May 2001

All rights reserved.
Copyright © 2001 by Netco Partners.
NETFORCE is a registered trademark of Netco Partners, a partnership
of Big Entertainment, Inc., and CP Group.
The NETFORCE logo is a registered trademark of Netco Partners, a
partnership of Big Entertainment, Inc., and CP Group.
This book, or parts thereof, may not be reproduced
without permission.
For information address: The Berkley Publishing Group,
a division of Penguin Putnam Inc.,
375 Hudson Street, New York, New York 10014.

The Penguin Putnam Inc. World Wide Web site address is
www.penguinputnam.com

ISBN: 0-425-17879-X

BERKLEY JAM BOOKS®
Berkley Jam Books are published by The Berkley Publishing Group,
a division of Penguin Putnam Inc.,
375 Hudson Street, New York, New York 10014.
BERKLEY JAM and its logo
are trademarks belonging to Penguin Putnam Inc.

PRINTED IN THE UNITED STATES OF AMERICA

10 9 8 7 6 5 4 3 2 1

We'd like to thank the following people, without whom this book would have not been possible:

Martin H. Greenberg, Larry Segriff, Denise Little, and John Helfers at Tekno Books; Mitchell Rubenstein and Laurie Silvers at Hollywood.com; Tom Colgan of Penguin Putnam Inc.; Robert Youdelman, Esquire; and Tom Mallon, Esquire. As always, we would like to thank Robert Gottlieb without whom this book would not have been conceived. We much appreciated the help.

I

Maybe the cab was an extravagance. We didn't have a client, and my boss, the great Lucullus Marten, might decide I was wasting his money. On the other hand, my feet were aching, and I could prop them up on the jump seat of the big, roomy Checker cab. People call me Marten's legman, and maybe they're right. Mainly, what I do is a lot of footwork, and that's what I was doing right now—checking libraries to find a copy of the Social Register, walking over to the offices of the New York Chronicle to read back files on the Van Alst family . . . and to check for any unpublished poop on the Van Alst murder.

Pamela Van Alst had been in Marten's office just days before, brought in by a friend who didn't like the crowd the poor little rich girl was running with. Marten doesn't like young females. He growled at her. Pamela didn't like opinionated detective geniuses who need a special chair to hold their oversized bulk. She left. Then she turned up dead last night. It was a particularly ugly way to go—she'd been dragged down a country road.

The killing had finally stirred Marten off his big, fat . . . laurels. Taking the murder as a personal insult, he'd sent me out to gather, as he put it, "the relevant information."

That's the Lucullus Marten method of cracking a case. He stays in the slightly drafty, gray stone mansion way west on Seventy-second Street, eating gourmet meals, drinking at least seven bottles of sparkling cider a day, and tending his world-class crop of cacti on the top floor. His trusty legman, Monty Newman—that's me—goes forth to track down facts, ask questions, and annoy suspects.

I report. He stores the info in a brain at least as massive as the rest of him, and comes up with solutions to the knottiest mysteries.

Unfortunately, the information I was coming home with, while relevant, wasn't very helpful. I could have dug much the same facts out of the newspaper coverage. And, thanks to the wealthy Van Alsts putting up an enormous reward to find the murderer of their beloved daughter, I'd already encountered several other investigators pushing into the case.

Simply put, the facts were as follows: The deceased had been found on a back road of Alstenburgh, an upstate town where the elite meet to raise property values. The discoverer had been a dairy farmer rushing his milk to market.

Pamela Van Alst had last been seen in the company of Woodrow Peyton, eldest son of a political dynasty. The Peytons had provided the nation with several senators and would-be presidents. Young Woodrow spent his time in Alstenburgh, Albany, Washington . . . and, often enough, on the more easygoing streets of Manhattan.

Society pages described him as "a young man-about-town." Newspapers are wary of libel suits. However, when I asked, the staffs of selected hotels, restaurants, and nightclubs called Woodie Peyton a bum—but a bum with a whole lot of money behind him.

I could have figured as much from the rather careful

way he was treated in the front-page news stories. So I'm afraid I had more weeds than flowers in the bouquet I was bringing back to Marten.

I stepped from the cab, carefully jotting the fare down in my notebook, and started for the iron-railinged steps of the house I know best in this city.

Then I noticed the beefy character coming out of a parked car, heading my way, and reaching into the light topcoat he wore against the late fall chill.

My own hand slipped under my jacket. I'd learned long ago that murder cases can turn quite unexpectedly ugly. A little artillery can go a long way in meeting some of those surprises.

The beefy man's meaty fingers emerged with nothing more deadly than a leather case, flashing a badge and an identification card. I hadn't pegged him as a member of the local law, and he wasn't. The ID was federal. I had a genuine G-man keeping me from the comforts of home.

"You're Monty Newman," he announced.

I shook my head in wonder. "The government's always right."

The beefy features contracted into a look that was supposed to scare me. "Let's say the government keeps an eye open for potential troublemakers. You've spent the day asking prying questions about some very important people."

"I wasn't aware that was against federal law," I said. "No state secrets were revealed, and none of us discussed overthrowing the established order. We're all waiting to see how the next elections work out."

"Very funny." The G-man sounded as if he'd been told humor was unpatriotic. "But certain people won't be laughing."

"Well, you certainly aren't," I had to agree. "I thought they'd managed to weed all you patronage types out of the feds. Certain people might frown on an officer running political errands, Agent Olin."

I'd already gotten his name when he flashed his cre-

dentials. Quick eyes were part of my job. The rest is just the way I am. When somebody pushes, I like to shove right back.

Olin twisted his face out of its previous unpleasant expression into an equally unpleasant sneer. "I don't think you'll get far—trying that, or staying on the Van Alst case."

Whoever he had behind him, Olin obviously thought he had ironclad protection. He had also decided not to waste any more time on me. "Remember what I told you . . . and pass it along to that fat freak inside."

I turned my back on this representative of the power and majesty of the law.

"Oh, count on it," I told him. "But I'll give you fair warning. You might need reinforcements if you're hoping to budge Lucullus Marten."

As the town house door swung closed behind Monty Newman, Matt Hunter disengaged from the computer program. He blinked for a moment, lying back in his computer-link couch. It took a little while to recover from the differences between the created world of the simulation and everyday reality. The sim was set in 1930s Manhattan—far away in time and space from the Washington, D.C., of 2025.

His room was a lot colder than the late fall chill of the sim. He'd left his window open, and the winter breeze coming in was downright freezing. The capital was in the grip of a cold spell. Forecasters were predicting snow, something that D.C. usually handled badly during its rare appearances.

Matt fought back a shiver as he went to shut the window. His jeans and long-sleeved T-shirt were much lighter than Monty Newman's snazzy wool suit. Right now, he wouldn't even have minded wearing the unpleasant Agent Olin's topcoat.

Matt's usually cheerful face set in a frown at the thought of a federal agent being set up as his opponent—

maybe even as a bad guy—in the sim. He knew several FBI people—specifically the special agents assigned to keep the country's computer networks free of criminals. Olin was nothing like the Net Force agents Matt had encountered.

The sound of a HoloNews broadcast filtering through the door of his room sent Matt glancing at the clock on the wall. His breath hissed through his teeth. *I was in longer than I should have been,* he thought. *Mom and Dad are home already. I'll really have to blow through my homework and supper if I want to hit the Net Force Explorers meeting tonight.*

Leif Anderson sighed. *Whenever I come early to a meeting, I always wind up regretting it.* He glanced around the featureless government-issue meeting space. As virtual constructs went, it was pretty basic—just a place to pop up after you'd synched in to your computer and given the address for the monthly meeting of the Net Force Explorers. It did have one nice touch—the meeting room always managed to grow seamlessly as more and more members turned up from all over the country. But other than that the scenery was strictly low rent. Still, he'd hoped to show up early, run into a few of his friends, and spend some time happily shooting the breeze with them. Things hadn't exactly worked out that way.

Actually, Leif had really just wanted to get out of the condo his family used as home base when they were in Washington. It was okay when he came down with his father to do some deals in the capital. But this time around, his mom was in the condo, too . . . and there just didn't seem to be enough room for all of them. Usually, Natalya Anderson stayed in New York when Dad had business in D.C. Or she went to London, Paris, St. Petersburg—wherever the dance world had a major outpost.

Her interest in dance wasn't surprising. After all, before Leif was born, she'd risen to stardom as Natalya Ivanova, dancing with one of the world's best ballet companies.

This week she was in Washington to see students performing for a local troupe. No stars, no big names . . . most likely none of these dancers was ever going to make it to any of the leading companies. But the choreographer for the troupe was one of Mom's old dancing partners, and he was premiering a new piece. As a consequence, Leif's mom was taking this very personally.

Before she left for the performance, if the state of her nerves was anything to go by, Leif would have thought his mom would be out there dancing herself instead of sitting in the audience. A little distance from the rare appearance of his mom in prima donna mode had seemed advisable.

Leif had finally fled to his computer, heading early to the Net Force Explorers meeting . . . and a little peace.

He hadn't gotten any, though. The first person to arrive had been Megan O'Malley. "You made the society news today," she announced. "Nice picture of you and your folks arriving in town."

She gave him a piercing look. "I've always suspected you edited your Net image. The holo showed a real-life zit on your chin."

Things rapidly went downhill from there. Leif couldn't understand it. He *liked* Megan. She was attractive, smart, a little sharp-tongued, but then, so was he. He'd missed her over the winter holidays. Instead of getting down to D.C., as he usually did, he'd been drafted for some social duty by his father and had been forced to stay in New York. Magnus Anderson had been forging a business alliance with Hardaway Industries, and Leif had been stuck as the holiday escort for Courtney Hardaway.

In a word, it had been disastrous. Leif had found himself comparing Courtney to Megan—sort of like trying to compare a spoiled and yapping miniature poodle to a playful but possibly lethal Doberman. Courtney was all facade—pleasant to Leif when their parents were around but miserably stuck-up otherwise. During their first moments alone, she'd let Leif know that she considered him way beneath her notice, hopelessly outclassed.

After all, Leif's dad was the one who'd amassed the Anderson family fortune, not some long-forgotten distant ancestor. That made Leif a social climber.

Shirtsleeves to shirtsleeves in three generations, Leif thought. *My generation is supposed to be the one that blows the money.*

On the other hand, the Hardaways had held on to their family loot for more than four generations . . . not counting the current influx of cash on its way from Anderson Investments Multinational.

The deal was now done, and Leif had been glad to get down to Washington. He'd even had hopes of actually meeting Megan someplace outside of veeyar—until she had popped up at this meeting and begun serving him hot-and-cold running attitude.

Apparently, *he* was the snob for not getting in touch with her over the holidays. One word led to another, until now they were down to the third-grade level—the "Did not!"/"Did too!" stage of the argument.

Leif never expected to be happy to see Andy Moore turn up. The crew's jokester usually managed to annoy Leif as often as he entertained him. But at least Andy diverted some of Megan's bad temper today.

David Gray was the next to link in. He was the calm, scientific member of the group. Leif had noticed that lately his friend looked happier in veeyar than in person. David's real-life self was currently hobbling around on a cane, thanks to a broken leg—a nasty souvenir from a recent adventure. The virtual David stepped lively to pull Leif away from the throng while Andy teased Megan into a murderous fury.

"What's going on with O'Malley?" Leif asked. "She just about bit my head off when I arrived."

"I hear she's angry with the world right now," David said quietly. "Especially with anyone she suspects of owning his own tuxedo."

Leif stared. "What?"

"This guy asked Megan to the Winter Formal—a Leet."

Even though he didn't go to Bradford Academy, Leif recognized the school slang. The Leets were the elite—the social in-crowd. Bradford was a good school that attracted students from the families of the wealthy, the politically powerful, and from Washington's diplomatic community. The date—especially for a Bradford formal dance—would have been a big deal for Megan. "What happened?"

"Guy blew her off at the last minute. His folks hooked him up with this other girl . . . from their circle." David's face looked as if he'd detected a bad smell.

"Megan got stuck with a gown?"

David nodded. "And no date. Moore wound up taking her—in this awful rented tux that he thought was a clever joke and Megan thought was the most embarrassing thing she'd ever laid eyes on. The Leet who'd started the whole mess snubbed her publicly at the dance, and nasty rumors about why he did that started flying all over school the next day."

"Oh." Now Leif was glad he hadn't explained why he hadn't exactly been available over the holidays. Talk about pouring oil on the fires . . .

"Why, here's another hero deciding to grace us with his appearance," Megan said sourly as Matt Hunter popped into existence beside them.

Matt half-turned. "I can always go," he said.

"What? And leave us alone with her?" Andy dropped to his knees, his hands up in a begging gesture. "No! *Pleeeeeease!*" Megan looked about ready to cut him down to that size permanently—and she had the martial-arts know-how to do it, too.

Matt made an attempt to head off any bloodshed. "Hey, I'm sorry if I haven't been around much lately. I got wrapped up in this really cool sim."

Arguments were forgotten as everybody clustered around. The Net—with all its possibilities and opportunities to have fun—was the reason these kids had joined the Net Force Explorers. If one member of the crew happened onto something good, the others all wanted in on it.

"I hope this is better than that kayaking-down-the-Matterhorn sim that Andy turned up," Megan growled.

"Not quite as death-defying," Matt admitted. "It's a mystery sim."

"So what's the big deal?" Maj Green, who'd somehow managed to synch in unnoticed, wanted to know. "You can find them everywhere. There's a million and three commercial sites offering interactive investigations."

"This sim is different," Matt insisted. "It's not one of those big-business, one-size-fits-all setups. One guy programmed it, and he's running it single-handed."

"A boutique sim," Megan sniffed. "That means rip-off rates—or are you beta-testing for this guy?"

"Neither," Matt said. "Ed Saunders is a mystery buff. This is his first shot. And it's a real labor of love." He grinned. "There's a whole bunch of detectives who are competing to solve the case, and if you read a lot of classic mysteries, you'll recognize them."

"Homage," Leif said.

"Plagiarism," Megan contradicted. "I hope this clown isn't using any of my dad's characters." Her father was a well-known author of mystery novels.

"That reminds me," Leif said. "I picked up your father's latest. Is he really going to go through with a title for every letter in the alphabet with this character?"

"What?" Megan demanded. "You don't think he'll last long enough to make it all the way through?"

"I thought somebody else had used that gimmick." Andy ducked as Megan swung round at him.

"Gimmick?" she said. "You think my father relies on gimmicks to sell his work?"

"Let's just hope he gets up to X," David said. "I want to see what he uses for the title."

"About this sim. Can we check it out?" Maj asked.

"I don't know," Matt replied. "I think Ed has all the sleuths set up."

" 'Sleuths,' " Megan mocked.

"Well, it's set in the 1930s," Matt quickly explained. "Although I think some of the detectives may come from later eras."

"Maybe there are openings for bit players," David suggested. "Like cops." His father was a homicide investigator for the D.C. police.

"Or stool pigeons," Megan said, hooking a thumb at Andy Moore.

"I'll check with Ed," Matt promised. He had no chance to say more. While he and his friends had been talking, quite a crowd had gathered in the virtual meeting room. Now one wall vanished to reveal a small stage with a military-looking figure standing on it.

Even though he was now a civilian working for Net Force, one glance at Captain James Winters said "Marine." He faced the Net Force Explorers in a relaxed parade rest, his hands clasped behind his back as he gave his usual opening. "Welcome to the national meeting of the Net Force Explorers."

The captain smiled. "I'm happy to say I have nothing of particularly earth-shaking importance to report today. The Net is running as smoothly as we could hope. No emergencies or baffling mysteries."

As he spoke, Winters glanced over to where Matt and his friends stood. Matt sort of ducked his head. Well, they did have something of a reputation for leaping into Net Force cases. With nothing going on, at least that wasn't likely to happen this time around.

"This year marks the FBI's ninetieth birthday," Winters went on. "Although the Justice Department has had investigators since 1908, we didn't officially become the Federal Bureau of Investigation until July 1, 1935.

"To mark the anniversary, the Bureau is setting up some historical simulations. The first of them opens this week, commemorating the antigangster successes of the 1930s."

"The glory days of the G-men," Megan muttered. "Before the first director gave in to megalomania."

Matt couldn't help contrasting Captain Winters with the nasty, fleshy virtual G-man he'd encountered in Ed Saunders's sim. Even J. Edgar Hoover hadn't been that ugly. *I really have to have a little talk with Ed about his FBI agent,* he told himself. *The sooner, the better.*

2

Sometimes Matt's friends hung out after the official Net Force Explorers meetings, switching through the Net to one of the kids' virtual workspaces. Tonight, however, Matt headed straight back to his own computer domain. He wanted to see if he had a chance of catching Ed Saunders.

No sooner did he synch in to his own space—a slab of black-and-white marble floating unsupported in the night sky—than he saw that one of the items scattered across the flying desktop was blinking determinedly. It was the tiny sculpture of an ear—an icon for Matt's virtmail account. Somebody had contacted him.

Judging from the intensity of the blinking, the message appeared urgent.

Matt vocalized a command—he could have simply thought it, but speaking helped him to concentrate. The virtmail program projected the titles of his latest messages in the air in front of him. The urgent one had little virtual flames flickering around its edges. It came from Ed Saunders.

Old Ed must have been reading my mind, Matt thought.

He gave the command to play the message. But instead of the sim-master's face, letters appeared. *How bizarre.* Shrugging, Matt started to read. He blinked as the message floating before him sank in.

No link-ins to the sim until further notice, the words curtly announced. *I've been hit with several nasty letters from lawyers—of the "cease and desist" variety. Let's talk it out—tomorrow, six o'clock, my place.*

The bottom line of the message was a Net address.

Well, there goes the crew's chances for getting any walk-ons, Matt thought. *What's all this "cease and desist" stuff?*

Matt got his answer the next evening. With his homework finished and his parents both late for dinner, he was completely free for the virtual meeting. He linked in precisely at six, giving his computer Ed Saunders's Net address. In the course of the day he'd repeated it so often, he'd memorized it.

Closing his eyes, Matt found himself flung through a kaleidoscope of spinning lights, the vast glowing structures of cyberspace streaming past him. Matt swung suddenly and headed for a compact neon-adorned office building—the sort of virtual address a small-scale entrepreneur might use.

Some of these lesser operations were housed in featureless cubes. Ed Saunders, in keeping with his interest in the period, had found a site that looked like a building from a century before.

Another swoop, and Matt found himself standing in a shadowy virtual workspace. A huge half-moon window overlooked darkened, but definitely mean, streets. The traditional battered wooden desk stood in front of the window, just as it had for every movie detective from Sam Spade on. The walls of the office, however, rose three times the height of a man. They were completely covered with bookshelves holding everything from leather-bound volumes to tattered paperbacks. Matt squinted. Each book he focused on held the title of a famous mystery. High above, a ceiling fan revolved creakily, sending gusts of warm air down on Matt.

"And who are you?" a nasal voice inquired from behind him.

Matt turned around to find the one element that didn't fit in this combination detective's office and library. A tall, skinny guy now sat behind the desk. Lank blond hair fell across his high, pale forehead. A pair of washed-out blue eyes stared at Matt from behind wire-framed glasses. Ed Saunders—who else could it be?—wasn't exactly up on the latest fashions. His shirt was a color that had never occurred in nature, and his bony wrists stuck out of too-short sleeves. Matt would have bet that the cuffs of Saunders's pants were a tad short, too.

The storklike nerd behind the desk asked again, "And you are . . . ?"

"Matt Hunter. In the sim, I'm—"

"Monty Newman, yes." The sim creator looked even more like a bird as he cocked his head to one side. "I have to say, you're a bit younger than I expected."

Matt didn't know how to answer that. His first step toward getting into the sim had been filling out a pretty comprehensive online questionnaire. Ed Saunders had asked about Matt's knowledge of the mystery field, what historical eras he liked, and lots of personal data, including how old he was. Matt had entered his proper age. If stork-boy here couldn't pay attention—

Right then another figure appeared in the office—a tall, thick, balding man who supported his massive weight on a thick ebony cane. A perfectly tailored black suit covered his bulk, and his face was square rather than jowly. But he was definitely a heavy man, the image of Lucullus Marten, reclusive private eye. In fact, he was the Lucullus Marten whom Matt worked with as Monty Newman.

A second later a tall, slender, hawk-faced man appeared. He also had a cane, a thin bamboo accessory which he leaned against negligently as his sharp blue eyes took in the room. "Milo Krantz," he announced in a clipped voice.

An instant after that a couple popped into existence on the other side of the room. They, too, were dressed in 1930s finery. The man wore a tuxedo. He had a thin mustache on a good-humored face—except for a certain ruthlessness in his gray eyes. The woman wore a white silk evening gown, her short-cropped brown hair bobbing as she glanced inquisitively around.

Both raised martini glasses.

"Mick and Maura Slimm have arrived," the man announced.

Matt nodded grimly. He'd read about the Slimms— and Krantz—in the sim's *New York Chronicle*. The three of them were considered "society sleuths."

Last to appear was a burly guy in a shabby trench coat. His tight pink face boasted a broken nose, and the big, hamlike hands sticking out from the coat's sleeves had scars all over the knuckles. Matt had already encountered him in the sim—Spike Spanner, hard-boiled private eye. He'd been making the same rounds as Monty Newman, gathering information.

Spanner took in the scene around him with angry bloodshot eyes. "How come them bozos got a drink and the rest of us got nothing?" he demanded in a hoarse voice.

"We brought our own, darling," Maura Slimm replied in a chirpy voice.

Spanner half-leaned against Ed Saunders's desk, opening drawers. "There oughta be a bottle stashed someplace. Since you invited us here, you should offer us a drink." He glanced at Matt. "None for the kid, though. Unless he can handle it."

"You've met the young man," Saunders said. "Although you know him as Monty Newman."

The other participants in the sim stared at Matt until he felt as though he were standing in his underwear.

Lucullus Marten's look was more like a glare. He was apparently angry with his erstwhile assistant for showing up as his real self rather than in the sim's proxy appearance. Shrugging, Matt vocalized a command and turned into Monty Newman.

A little belatedly, he thought he realized why the others had all attended this meeting in their sim personas. They didn't want to give anything away to their competitors. Now it appeared that Lucullus Marten thought his chances of being first to solve the case had been hurt. The other players knew his legman was just a teenage kid instead of a thirty-something sophisticate.

Even Marten hadn't realized that until this moment, Matt suddenly realized. *Unless he's been hacking into Saunders's application files.*

Maybe it was just as well he hadn't known. The fat man was unbearable enough under normal conditions. If he now thought he had a reason to rag on Matt . . . well, the sim might just be a bit more complicated going forward.

Ed Saunders interrupted his thoughts. "Give up on the bottle, Spanner. I called this meeting because of a real-life problem. In the last two weeks I've received nasty letters from several lawyers—not ambulance chasers, but partners in big law firms. What you might call power brokers."

"You mentioned somebody wanting you to cease and desist—" Matt began.

"Quiet, boy," Lucullus Marten cut in. His colorless eyes bored into Ed Saunders's face. "Why should anyone have a problem with this . . . harmless entertainment?"

"There are people who apparently don't think it's harmless," Saunders said angrily. He hunched his shoulders, resting his hands on the desk. Much of his anger, it seemed, was aimed at himself. "I based this mystery scenario heavily on an actual case. I thought it was long enough ago that nobody would care."

"You mean this was for real?" Spike Spanner growled.

"Some rich dame actually got herself ground into chopped meat?"

Maura Slimm waved an empty martini glass at Saunders. "Naughty, naughty. We don't know that yet—unless you were cheating?"

"Judging from the lawyers' communications, you certainly miscalculated the amount of disinterest on the part of the affected parties," Milo Krantz said in a dry voice. "That raises an interesting point. How was your work discovered? While it is of paramount interest to those of us here"—he gestured around the circle of make-believe sleuths—"your divertissement would not, I imagine, be well known in the wider world."

"It made me wonder, too," Saunders said grimly. "When the first letters came, I just kept my head down. Figured it might blow over. This latest letter explained a little more. The timing was just great. It came just after my bank called in my college loan."

His gaze was accusing as he looked at the simulated sleuths. "It seems that somebody—most likely one of you—remembered or came across a reference to the case I was using. Then that somebody began hacking into sealed court records about the case. That set off some alarms in high places, and got the—"

Saunders bit off his words before he gave away the actual name. "It got a very important family—and their lawyers—on my back."

"Hacking?" Spanner hooked his thumbs in his belt. "That kinda egghead stuff ain't up my line."

"I'm offended that you would include me in such insinuations," Milo Krantz said.

"Maura and I just came along for the fun of it all." Mick Slimm gave everyone a lazy smile.

"While I don't appreciate your suspicions, I can understand them." Lucullus Marten's scowl grew thunderous. "I can assure you that I have taken no such actions." He glanced at Matt. "Though I cannot necessarily claim to control the youthful enthusiasm of my associate."

"Hey!" Matt angrily responded to the veiled accusation. "The only digging I've been doing has been inside the sim. You know that."

"Unless," Marten rumbled, "you dream of stealing the credit for this case from your own employer?"

"Shocking," Krantz sniffed.

"I guess that's what happens when you have to rely on everything coming to you second-hand." Maura Slimm raised a perfect eyebrow as she looked at Marten.

"Maybe if you got off that fat duff of yours—" Spanner began.

Still hunched at his desk, Ed Saunders rubbed an obviously aching head. "I'd hoped that whoever was responsible would own up—and promise to stop." He looked around at the circle of odd characters. "Obviously, that's not going to happen with everybody here, and accusations and arguments will get us nowhere. So I'll put it this way. Until the hacker contacts me—privately—and gives his word that all further hacking will stop, the sim stays down."

He sighed. "With nothing to win, there shouldn't be any reason for anybody to poke around in the real case."

Leif Anderson shook his head as Matt told him about Ed Saunders's meeting. "Sounds like your friend Saunders is hopelessly naive." Leif stretched out on the Danish Modern Revival couch in his simulated living room. Most people created a one-room virtual space. Leif had gone for something bigger—a simulated Icelandic stave house, with ever-changing scenes in the windows. This visit Matt could see a volcano erupting in the distance. Knowing Leif, it was undoubtedly a full-scale, authentic recreation of some actual Icelandic volcano in action—and Leif had probably paid somebody well to provide the touch.

"What would you have done?" Matt was a little annoyed. But then, Matt had the reputation of being the crew's straight arrow, and probably deserved it.

"I'd have avoided using a real case in the first place. Some lawyers spend their lives looking for trouble they can profit on. Failing that, I'd probably have let the sim go on—and kept an eye out for anyone trying to use information I hadn't given them," Leif said.

"Not so easy to wait for somebody to trip up with a bunch of lawyers and a bank breathing down your neck." Matt scowled. "Not that you'd know how that feels."

"Hah! Maybe I don't have to worry about money, but I've had lawyers after me before for various things," Leif replied, stung. "And you know it. I'm a fat lawsuit target. Being rich isn't always a bowl of cherries all the time."

"No, especially not if it means getting killed." Matt frowned, obviously thinking about the case behind the mystery sim he'd been playing in. "It's weird to think a girl actually died the way I heard about it in the sim."

Leif looked at him knowingly. "And you'd like to find out more."

"Maybe," Matt admitted.

Leif's smile grew broader. "So what brings you to Uncle Leif instead of an information-meister like David Gray?"

"Apparently asking questions about the case on the Net starts somebody's spiderwebs jangling," Matt said. "I figure the last thing my folks want to see is a 'cease and desist' letter from some lawyer."

"And instead, you figure on checking out my knowledge of society gossip and scandal—even though the story may turn out to be ancient." Leif couldn't hold back a chuckle. "Guess I should be touched by your faith in me. But I warn you—even I get a little hazy once we get before the Girl on the Red Velvet Swing."

Matt blinked. "The who?"

Leif sighed. "Sorry. Just showing off. It was a primo scandal in its day. All the elements—a showgirl turned society bride, fooling around with a famous society architect. Her husband was a rich psycho who shot the architect dead in front of a crowd—and still got off, thanks to his family's money."

"And this was when?"

"The Stanford White killing goes back to 1906. His killer, Harry K. Thaw, enjoyed catered meals from the best restaurant in New York City while he was in jail. He spent less than ten years in various mental institutions—and lived until 1947."

"And how is this useful?"

Leif felt his face getting warm. "I told you I was showing off."

Matt simply shook his head. "Let's hope the death of this girl is a little more recent." He began reciting to Leif the details he'd collected as Monty Newman.

"Priscilla Hadding." The words burst out after Leif had listened for only a couple of minutes, interrupting Matt's account. "It happened over in Delaware. Big news at the time. She belonged to an old-line society family. Got killed right before the debutante ball." He nodded. "The police never figured out who dragged her to her death."

"How long ago was this?" Matt wanted to know. "Delaware isn't all that far away. And if a big political name was also attached to the case, it wouldn't have just faded away."

"This is Washington," Leif reminded him. "Lots of scandals under the bridge since the Hadding case."

He squinted up at the ceiling, trying to get his dates straight. "It happened way before we were born. Got to be more than forty years, now." Bringing his gaze back to Matt, Leif shrugged. "Call it a lost chapter of the Callivant Curse."

3

"The *Callivant* Callivants?" Matt asked numbly. Of course he knew the name. The Callivants were one of America's great political dynasties, up there with the Tafts of Ohio and the Kennedys of Massachusetts.

Like the Tafts and Kennedys, the Callivants had given the nation senators and congressmen. Unlike those other dynasties, the Callivants had never succeeded in reaching the White House. Steve Callivant, the candidate the family had been grooming, had died in the Gulf War. His brother Will, a decorated veteran, had entered presidential primaries—and perished when his campaign bus overturned. The youngest brother, Martin, made a stab at the next presidential election cycle—only to have his bid cut short by a terrorist bomb.

The politics of tragedy seemed to dog the Callivants. Attempting to hide the effects of a stroke, Senator Walter Callivant had tried the experimental Patel Procedure. The controversial treatment had failed disastrously, leaving the senator wheelchair-bound. Riding on a wave of sympathy both for the senator and over Martin's assassination, Walter's son, Walter G. Callivant, had moved into his father's Senate seat.

Matt had been aware of some of the media coverage there. Walter G. had turned out to be a patch of low comedy in the family tapestry. Although he tried to distinguish himself with the middle initial, people always called him Junior—or worse, Callivant Lite. He'd ended up a one-term wonder after six years of providing all too much material for the late-night comics.

Still, the Callivants came and went to their compound on the outskirts of Wilmington, pulling strings in Delaware's state capital, Dover . . . and also in Washington. A new generation of Callivant cousins had provided a couple of promising young congressmen.

Callivants were always generous with their celebrity for charitable causes—the more glittering the party, the better. They could be depended upon to attend society shindigs, and always, always for political performances—especially ones commemorating the family's honored dead.

How could a Callivant have been involved in the death of this girl—what was her name? Priscilla Hadding?

When Matt asked, Leif gave him another shrug. "As the cops say, she was last seen in the company of Walter G. Callivant."

"The senator?" Matt couldn't believe what he was hearing.

"His election was well off in the future at that time," Leif explained. "We're talking early 1980s, here. Walter G. was busy squeaking through prep school with a gentleman's C average. Silly—that, by the way, was Priscilla's personal choice for a nickname—was debating whether to spend her senior year abroad."

"So they were just about our age when this happened." To Matt, the story seemed weirder and weirder.

"Yep. The night Priscilla Hadding disappeared, there was a big end-of-school party. Half the rich kids from Delaware, Maryland, Virginia—and D.C.—put in an appearance. It was on the back forty of somebody's estate. There was a big bonfire, lots of kids paired off, and apparently, people brought in lots of refreshments." Leif's face twisted. "I've been to parties like that. 'Party' is putting it very politely. 'Drunken brawl' might come closer. If Silly Hadding was last seen with Walter G., depend on it that the eyewitnesses had pretty blurry vision. Anyway, according to the papers of the day, the witnesses disagreed on the time, the place, and how the two kids were getting along. Conspiracy theorists like to think it was a smoke screen engineered by the all-powerful Callivant family."

Leif laughed. "Others think it's just another campaign in the secret war *against* the Callivants. The Invisible Masters of Evil killed Will and Martin, crippled Walter Senior, and tried to smear Walter G."

"And what do you think?" Matt asked.

"I don't like either extreme. Enough strange, sad, and stupid things happen to any family over generations. When the family is famous, the media tends to play up those events. On the other hand, rich families can afford the kind of lawyers who lay down a smoke screen as a matter of course. And a lot of police forces aren't exactly gung-ho about investigating prominent pillars of the local community."

"What did Walter G. have to say?"

"When the cops finally talked to him—he was in a private hospital for shock or a hangover or something—Walter G. wasn't very helpful. He said he and Silly made out a little—they were a semicouple, as I recall—then they split up, and young master Callivant drove home."

"He didn't take Silly—the girl—home first?" Matt felt silly, using that upper-crust nickname. And he couldn't believe that any boy would leave a girl stranded at a party, no matter how ritzy.

"Apparently, she wanted to stay." Leif turned to his friend with an odd expression on his face. "You've never been to that kind of party—and you should probably be glad. The rich really are different, in one way especially. They're very fond of getting their own way. The two kids may have had an argument, and one or the other went storming off. It could even have happened the way young Callivant told it. The girl could have dismissed him. 'Run along, now. I've got other fish to fry.' "

"You make it sound—*so* unpleasant," Matt couldn't help saying.

"I told you," Leif said, his mocking smile completely gone. "Being rich is no bowl of cherries."

He lounged back on his uncomfortable-looking seat. "So, now that you've gotten some of the gory details— and a whole lot of conjecture—what are you going to do with the information?"

Now it was Matt's turn to shrug. "I have no idea," he confessed. He held up his hand. "No. One thing I do know. I won't be detecting very much in that sim, unless the player who's been snooping around confesses to Ed Saunders."

"I hope you're not holding your breath on that possibility," Leif told him. "Otherwise, you'll end up looking like this." He frowned for a moment in thought, then his face turned bright blue. It was one of the joys of being on the Net—virtual special effects on command.

"You don't think the hacking will stop?" Matt asked.

"Oh, it may stop," Leif replied. "But I can't see anyone admitting to it. After seeing what happened to your pal Saunders, do you think these guys are going to nominate themselves as targets for the Callivant lawyers' brigade?"

Leif had almost forgotten Matt's visit as he wrestled with the intricacies of tying a black silk bow tie. The Delmarva Club was strictly old-fashioned. Formal events meant black tie and tuxedo—even if it was an event for the "young people."

Looking in his mirror, Leif had to smile. He looked good in a monkey suit—although, he also had to admit, that was true enough for most males. His formal suit had been hand-tailored to make the most of his slim frame, and the red hair above his slightly sharp features glowed like a flame. The effect was that of a very well-dressed fox.

Leif bared his teeth at his reflection as the internal phone system sounded. It was the doorman, reporting that his ride had arrived.

Arriving downstairs from the penthouse, Leif stood for a second in disbelief. His pal Charlie Dysart had gone all-out for tonight's little excursion. The car was a classic, a beautiful vintage Dodge gleaming as if it had just come out of the showroom.

"Charlie, you've definitely outdone yourself," Leif said, shaking his head. "I know your dad collects cars, but how did you—"

"What Father doesn't know won't hurt him," replied young Dysart, in a rig even more resplendent than Leif's. His dark hair was slicked back in the manner of some long-forgotten flatfilm personality. "At least it won't hurt until he happens to check the odometer on this baby."

The trip from Washington to the Wilmington suburb of Haddington was about ninety miles. Yeah, that would put a sizable change on the mint car's mileage.

Leif got in. "By the way," Charlie said as they pulled away, "did I mention that you're paying for the gas?"

The winding country road made for a welcome relief from the interstate, where Charlie Dysart had done everything but play bumper cars with his father's valuable collector's item. Leif hoped he hadn't sweat through his tux.

The Dysarts were an old-money family who had invested well. Their family fortune had recently enlarged nicely, thanks to Leif's father. They spent their time on charity, hobbies, counting their money, and—in Charlie's case—being outrageous.

That was part of the reason Charlie'd invited Leif along for this road trip. The Delmarva Club was a fortress for the old, privileged families of Delaware, Maryland,

and Virginia, as the club name suggested. Members' families were expected to have fought prominently at least in the Civil War, if not in the Revolution. It was not a place where the firstborn son of an immigrant billionaire would be warmly welcomed.

Before his exciting ride, Leif had expected the evening to be deadly dull. Still, if Charlie wanted to rile the old-line members, the least Leif could do was go along with the plan.

Charlie had finally slowed down on the pitch-black country lane. Leif could barely make out the fieldstone wall to one side. Then, suddenly, he spotted light ahead, streaming through a pair of open iron gates. Charlie piloted the Dodge into a turn.

Gravel crunched under their wheels as they moved toward a pillared house that would have made a perfect set for a Civil War movie. They swept round a circular drive, where Charlie turned the car over to a valet parking attendent.

A moment later, they were inside the house, and sober-faced servants removed their overcoats as Charlie produced his invitation. Then they were heading into a ballroom.

The glittering crystal chandeliers were from another age, contrasting with the slightly shabby carpeting—typical of any WASP enclave—and the sedate clothing of the Delmarva Club's younger generation.

There was a band that managed to make any music it played seem twenty years older than it really was. And through some subtle magic—Leif's father called it "the cursed Society Beat"—there was no way to dance to the tunes.

The refreshments were, in finest Anglo-Saxon tradition, tasteless and also nonalcoholic. Leif was sure there was some spot outside, away from the eyes of the chaperones, where discreet hip flasks appeared.

Those chaperones, by the way, were congregated against the rear wall of the large room, looking about as bored as Leif felt—except for one older woman. She stood ramrod stiff, her short white hair in striking contrast to the black dress she wore. Her eyes seemed to glitter as she greedily took in the sight of the dancing teenagers.

Charlie Dysart followed Leif's gaze. "Creepy, huh? That's old Felicia Hadding. The town's named after her family. For more than forty years, they tell me, she's turned up at every youth party. Always the same. Dressed in black, and ready to jump on anyone who does anything out of line."

Leif stood very still as a couple of other facts came swimming up from his memory—bits of the long-ago case that he hadn't told Matt. Priscilla Hadding had died on a back-country road in the society hamlet of Haddington, Delaware. And her mother had been a widow named Felicia Hadding.

"Any reason for that?" Leif asked through suddenly dry lips.

Charlie shrugged. "She lost her pride and joy in some accident after a party. I don't know why she doesn't join one of those groups against drunk drivers instead of ruining everyone's fun."

"Maybe she wouldn't like the publicity," Leif said. Old-line society types felt the only times their name should appear in the papers were when they were born, when they were married, and when they died.

He paused, hit by a sudden notion. Matt automatically assumed—and so had he—that the cease-and-desist letters came from the Callivants. What if those lawyers were instead working for Felicia Hadding? Maybe she didn't want anyone nosing around in the facts about her daughter's death.

"Whoa!" Charlie Dysart's boisterous comment cut through Leif's thoughts. "Looks like we get to party with the rich and *famous* tonight! That's Nikki Callivant coming off the dance floor."

Talk about your coincidences, Leif thought. *After talk-*

ing about that old case with Matt, I come to Haddington and meet a Callivant.

On second thought, it might not be such a big coincidence after all. The Callivant compound wasn't all that far from Haddington. And this was probably the sort of society affair that the young Callivants were encouraged to attend.

He knew the name Nicola Callivant. She was Walter G.'s granddaughter, about the same age as Leif and Matt. Either she wasn't interested or wasn't old enough for the splashier affairs attended by her older cousins. Somehow, she'd managed to keep away from the lenses of the press and HoloNews.

The few pictures Leif had seen of her made Nicola look fragile, like an overly nervous thoroughbred horse. In holos her features seemed too delicate, her expression too refined.

The word you're looking for, Leif told himself, *is effete.*

Seeing Nikki in real life changed that impression. Yes, her face was delicate, more delicate even than portraits of her mother, a famed beauty. Her hair was light brown and fine, floating like a cloud around her face. But those deep blue, almost violet, eyes were far from delicate. They glittered with pride, and with intelligence Leif could feel even halfway across the room.

Without even discussing it, Leif and Charlie began heading toward the girl. Nicola gave the guy she'd been dancing with a cool smile and began turning away.

"Hey! Nikki!" Charlie Dysart called, grabbing Leif by the arm. "I didn't think you'd be out slumming tonight."

Nikki Callivant's lips retained the same smile, but Leif noticed a brief flicker in her eyes. He recognized the look. Sometimes it passed between his Net Force friends when Andy Moore got a little too boisterous.

"Hello, Dysart," she said, her voice flat.

"I want you to meet a friend of mine," Charlie said, drowning out her words. "Leif, say hello to Nikki."

Dysart's crude introduction left Leif no choice. He'd just have to make the best of an embarrassing situation. "Ms. Callivant, how do you do. I'm Leif Anderson—"

Those incredible eyes suddenly went cold. "I've heard about you, Anderson."

Leif almost physically stumbled. "Excuse me?" You'd think he'd broken wind instead of trying to break the ice.

"You pestered a friend of mine," Nicola Callivant spoke remorselessly on. "Forced your company on her. Embarrassed her. Do you speak French, Mr. Anderson? Maybe you'll understand a few of the words she had to say about you. *Parvenu. Arriviste.*"

As she spoke, Leif couldn't help noticing the fine-boned sculpting of Nikki Callivant's nose—even though she was looking down it at him.

"Déclassé," she finally concluded her insulting list.

Leif's French was impeccable, better than hers was if the accent was anything to go by. He understood each painful word. Social climber. Upstart. Lower class.

"So who had all these nice things to say about me?" he asked in a carefully level tone of voice.

Nikki Callivant's right eyebrow rose in a perfect arch. "Is it a hobby of yours? Are there so many women who might say such things that you can't guess? Do you push yourself on every woman you meet?"

"It's an exercise in masochism."

The girl's lips twisted in disgust. "A friend of mine from New York. Courtney Hardaway."

Leif spread his hands. "Well, there you go. Courtney *did* have to put up with me. Just as I had to put up with her. We were forced together by my parents—and by hers. Hardaway Industries was getting a big cash transfusion from my dad's company." He made a modest, waving-away gesture. "Yes, I know. Crude. New money. Not like yours. But then, my father had certain handicaps. His family was busy being oppressed while your family was busily war profiteering during World War Two."

Beside him, Leif heard Charlie Dysart make a noise somewhere between a gasp and a gulp.

Nicola Callivant showed her breeding, however. First, her perfect face went pale as marble. Then her cheeks burned bright red. "How dare you!" she grated. "I am a Callivant!"

"And I'm an Anderson," Leif replied. "Thanks for teaching me an important lesson. I wouldn't have believed it. But there are worse snobs on this earth than Courtney Hardaway."

Spinning on his heel, he stalked away.

4

.

The moons of Jupiter continued their stately orbital dance around the swollen bulk of their mother planet. Megan O'Malley took a long minute to study the view from her seat in the stone amphitheater cut into the crust of Ganymede. This was her personal virtual space, big enough to hold the largest crowd—like all her friends from the Net Force Explorers.

She finally brought her eyes down to stare at the guest of honor in disbelief. "You actually dissed a Callivant—and lived?"

"There were a couple of tight moments," Leif Anderson admitted. "But I managed to get out of there before the lynch mob was able to find a rope."

Andy Moore laughed. "Even so, word will get out. I mean, what you did is like taking a whiz on the Washington Monument. Aren't you afraid your folks will get deported or something?"

Leif rolled his eyes. "Please."

Megan figured the subject of parents was probably a painful one for Leif right now. The Andersons had re-

turned late last night to find Leif not at home, long after
he was expected back from the party. They'd tried to
contact him on his wallet-phone—and had gotten no answer. So they'd called around to Leif's Washington
friends, waking up a lot of people, not finding their wan-
dering son . . . and, in the end, leading to this virtual
meeting of the crew, who had finally tracked Leif down,
at home, just before dawn. Everybody wanted to find out
what *really* happened.

So far, Megan had to admit, the story had been pretty
entertaining.

"So how come your folks couldn't get through to
you?" Maj Greene demanded.

Leif smiled, but his eyes moved just a little too much.
"My phone crapped out."

The needle on Megan's mental BS meter flicked. Leif
was *not* being honest. "How could that be? I thought you
had the top-of-the-line, latest-model, most expensive
wallet-phone known to humankind."

"Yeah. Maybe." Leif really didn't want to answer this.
"You'd think it would be waterproof."

"Water-resistant. It is. How'd you let it get wet enough
to kill it?" Megan hooted in derision.

"Can I help it if I ended up in a fountain, thanks to
some of Nikki's Neanderthal male friends? Do you know
how long it took for me to dry out?

"How could you let that happen?" David Gray asked
in disbelief. "Didn't you have any warning?"

Leif wouldn't meet their eyes. "Oh, I saw them coming. I just figured I could talk my way out of it."

"Yeah," Megan repeated, "like you did with Nikki Callivant, you silver-tongued devil." She shook her head.
"I'm beginning to believe that study on HoloNews—the
one that says ninety percent of problems result from human error."

"Forget about your folks being deported," Andy said
with a malicious grin. "How long would you last in the
Net Force Explorers if word of this got out?"

His tone was somewhere along the line of "Hey, rich boy, how much is our silence worth to you?"

Megan gave Andy a sharp look. "This from the genius who dragged a virus into the system for last month's meeting."

"How did you—" Andy began. He quickly shut up under the glares of everyone in the virtual hangout. "It was supposed to be a joke."

"Very funny, Moore," Maj Greene growled. "I wasted hours making sure nothing had infiltrated my system."

Matt Hunter, who'd been very quiet up to now, suddenly leaned forward. "What was this Nicola Callivant like?"

"Pretty snotty, it sounds like," Maj said flatly.

"Not a good first impression—on either of our parts, that's for sure," Leif agreed. Then he was looking up at the planetarium show overhead. "But she was surprising, too. Pictures don't do Nikki Callivant justice. They make her look like some kind of starved waif doll. But when you see her in person, there's something else . . . something more."

"Right," Andy Moore joked. "There's that rotten personality."

Megan didn't pay attention. She was giving silent commands to her computer. An instant later, Nicola Callivant's image floated in front of Megan, for her eyes only.

Leif had been surprisingly careful, not calling the girl pretty. But seeing her in a formal gown, that was exactly the word that came to Megan's mind. Nikki Callivant did look like a doll—a high-fashion model doll.

Megan struggled to keep her face still as she vented a sigh of frustration. *Looks like Leif's off on another wild chick chase,* she thought. *Boys and their hormones. What can you do with them? Even a thorough dunking didn't cool him off.*

Sooner or later, she was sure, Leif would come back to earth again—probably with a thud. She had seen the pattern often enough. The only problem was that the Callivant clan was tightly knit, not terribly kind to outsiders, and all too powerful.

If Leif decides to make a fool of himself over her, I hope he doesn't get any of the other guys involved.

She looked at him, still singing the praises of the girl who'd insulted him. *He can play with fire if he wants to, but I don't want anyone else burned.*

For Matt Hunter, Leif's story of the doings at the Delmarva Club gave a fascinating—and not too pleasant—peek into the world of the rich and powerful. Leif might joke about lynch mobs, but he had undoubtedly passed quite a few uncomfortable minutes after his run-in with Nicola Callivant.

That Charlie Dysart must be a real piece of work, Matt thought as the others began cheerfully ragging on Leif and Andy Moore. Matt couldn't imagine leaving a friend dangling in the wind—especially if he'd been responsible for putting the friend out there in the first place.

But that's what Dysart had done. Leif's ride home had suddenly vanished into the crowd, probably before Nikki Callivant's eyes could incinerate him or the well-soaked Leif could desecrate the upholstery of his collector car. He hadn't helped Leif. In fact, he seemed to have gone out of his way to pretend that he didn't even know him.

The club was a bad place to be—especially if you weren't exactly welcome, you were soaking wet, your ride had vanished, and your wallet-phone had picked that moment to die. Leif had finally dried off and called for a cab. The hit to his pride probably matched, if not exceeded, the damage to his Universal Credit Card account. A ride from Wilmington to Washington made for a hefty fare—especially since he'd have to pay for the cab's empty trip back as well.

Matt could just imagine Leif's comment as he got in the car: "Driver, I'm about to make you a wealthy man."

The rest of the night probably hadn't all been that humorous, Matt was ready to bet. Leif hadn't much gone into that. But he had mentioned that in the end he'd waited for the cab standing outside on the pillared porch, still slightly damp.

Apparently, the chill of a February night had been preferable to the deep-freeze atmosphere inside the ballroom. Megan, being her usual vengeful self, asked Leif what he was going to do about Dysart.

"We go to the same fencing club," Leif explained with a barbed smile. "Charlie is not going to enjoy his next practice bout with me."

Leif had been genuinely embarrassed as he begged his friends' pardon for the disturbance this latest escapade had caused them.

"I guess it's nice to know your parents care," Maj said.

"More than you know." Leif sighed. "That will be the last time I go out for a bit. I'm grounded for the foreseeable future. I'm not sure which they thought was worse—that I scared 'em by going missing, or what I was up to while I was missing. Dad's more interested in finance than keeping the family name out of the papers, but my mom—"

"Couldn't be happy about gaining a Callivant for an enemy," David finished. "It could even blow back on your father. The Callivants have lots of pull—"

Leif gave an unbelieving laugh. "You're as bad as Andy with that stupid deportation joke. I traded words with a teenage girl. What are they going to do about it?"

He was a little more serious as the group began breaking up. "Can I have a private word?" he whispered to Matt.

"Your place or mine?" Matt replied.

Moments later they switched from Megan's amphitheater to Matt's flying desktop. Grinning, Matt adopted the cross-legged lotus yoga position as he floated in the starry night sky. "What's up?"

"Just something I was reminded of during my evening in hell," Leif said. "I wasn't actually in Wilmington, but in a town outside the city boundaries—a place called Haddington."

Matt looked at his friend in puzzlement. "And what—"

Leif interrupted, breaking the town name in two. "HADDING-ton. As in a town founded by somebody named Hadding."

Matt realized his mouth was hanging open, so he shut it. "*Those* Haddings?"

"A bit of the story I'd forgotten," Leif admitted. "There was also a really strict chaperon keeping an eye on things. Charlie said she was the widow Hadding, who'd apparently lost a child to some sort of disaster."

"Pretty weird," Matt said. "Imagine stumbling over that place—and that lady—right after talking about it."

Leif nodded. "It reminded me that there are two families involved in the case—two *rich* families, both of whom can use high-priced lawyers."

"Why would the Haddings want to hush up all references to their daughter's death?"

"Some society families might consider murder somewhat . . . vulgar." Leif shrugged. "Go figure."

Matt took a moment to absorb what his friend was saying. "I guess that makes some sort of bizarre sense."

"I keep telling you, buddy, the rich are different," Leif said.

"What you're telling me now is that Ed Saunders may have the reclusive Haddings on his back instead of, or in addition to, the snotty Callivants." Matt threw out his arms. "More enemies—great! Well, it's unlikely that I'll have much chance to discuss the case with Ed. It's a dead matter now. He's pulled the plug on the sim."

As he spoke, one of the icon objects on his floating desktop began to glow—the ear.

"Looks like someone is trying to get in touch with you," Leif observed.

Matt picked up the icon and gave a command. A list of virtmail messages appeared in the air before him, urgent flames licking around an all-too-familiar name.

"Speak of the devil, as the old saying goes."

Leif craned his neck. The glowing letters were backward from his point of view. "Something from Saunders?"

Matt gave another command, and the floating message shifted to a position where they both could read it.

"Another meeting," Leif said.

"Because the hacking—excuse me, the 'attempts at unauthorized data extraction'—have continued." Matt gave his friend a look. "What is it with lawyers that they need five words to do the work of one?"

Leif shrugged. "What is it with your sim partners that one has to keep sticking his nose—"

"Or hers," Matt pointed out.

"You're showing a bit of lawyer there yourself," Leif joked. "That someone has to stick a gender-nonspecific unpleasant word where it has no business being stuck?"

Matt was rereading the virtmail message. "From the looks of the last paragraph, I'd say the mysterious client must be the Callivants." He pointed. "The Haddings might be able to threaten Ed the Stork with expulsion from the Social Register. But I think it would take Callivant clout to start an audit on the poor guy's back taxes."

Leif nodded. "You going to go to this meeting?" he asked.

"Kind of a waste, talking about a sim that's not going to happen anymore." He dismissed the message but didn't erase it. "After this tax thing, I'm *sure* Saunders won't want to work with us."

"Who are you kidding?" Leif said. "You've got a whole new mystery now. The Case of the Hidden Hacker."

Matt hated when people saw through him so easily. "All right, I'll probably check it out."

"Just be careful," Leif advised. "You guys are already being hit with taxes. Can death be far behind?"

•   •   •

I dressed with special care for tonight's meeting. It reminded me of the grand finales Lucullus Marten sometimes staged for the end of a case. More likely, though, this would turn out to be the sort of loud argument that usually happened when suspects were drawn, one way or another, into the great man's office.

Too bad Marten wouldn't have his special heavyweight chair to sit in.

I chose a bold—and expensive—silk tie that a wealthy lady friend had given me as a gift. It went well with the blue flannel suit I was wearing. While it was the best in my wardrobe, I figured Mick Slimm would probably appear in something more expensive. He was the kind of guy who'd think nothing of spending five hundred simoleons for a tasteful sport coat. Milo Krantz probably spent even more on his shoes. Spike Spanner could just as easily come in a saber-toothed tiger pelt—something to match his caveman personality.

It took two tries to get the knot the way I like it. I turned to the mirror and did the necessary with the military brushes, then slipped into my jacket. Enough with the preliminaries. I was ready for the main bout.

Matt pulled back from the Monty Newman persona, maintaining his appearance as a proxy image. At a silent command Newman's virtual bedroom vanished, to be replaced with Matt's floating workspace.

He knew why he'd let himself sink into the virtual character's confident, slightly smart-aleck style. Matt was nervous. It was ridiculous. He'd done nothing wrong. Why should he worry over what these people—rivals in a mystery sim—might be thinking about him? More than one of them seemed, as Monty Newman might say, "decidedly loony."

Why else would a hacker keep digging into the Hadding case after the fictional Van Alst murder had come to a crashing halt? It wasn't just useless, it was obviously painful for the Callivants—and definitely troublesome for Ed Saunders.

Matt allowed himself to arrive a few minutes late for this meeting, to find the other participants, all proxied up as their fictional sleuth counterparts, sitting in a circle around Saunders's desk.

Surprise, surprise. Lucullus Marten's mammoth chair had been included. The big man leaned on his cane, trying to get Maura Slimm out of its vastness—while also trying to avoid bursting a blood vessel.

"Young lady—" he began. The tone was unmistakable. It said, "I am no longer amused. In fact, I never *was* amused with you."

"Oh, Lukie," Maura's chirpy voice replied, "don't be a spoilsport."

"Let him have his seat, darling," Mick Slimm said.

"Yeah, give him a break," Spike Spanner put in. "Before he starts breakin' the furniture."

Marten settled his bulk in the big leather chair. Matt took a much smaller seat beside him.

"Mr. Saunders," Marten said, grabbing the role of spokesman, "I'm sure all of us here regret your additional troubles."

"All, apparently, but one," Milo Krantz interjected, the light from Saunders's desk lamp glinting off his spectacles. "I confess myself at a loss, however, as to the manner of finding that person."

"A fine bunch of sleuths we are," Mick Slimm joked.

"Yeah," Saunders said. "That's the problem." He looked less like a stork today and more like a hunted rabbit. "So here's what I'm going to do about it. I'm giving you people twenty-four hours. If the hacker hasn't contacted me by then, and agreed to stop this nonsense, I'm sending a virtmail to the lawyers, explaining that I've stopped the sim—and giving them a list of your actual identities."

"You can't do that!" A lot of the perkiness had dropped from Maura Slimm's voice. "Our privacy—"

"Was waived in the sim agreement you all signed," Saunders grimly replied. "You should have read the small print. It's just a form that I copied from the programming handbook, but now I'm glad I did. Maybe, if I cooperate with these people, they'll stop putting the screws to me and go looking where the trouble is really coming from."

It was almost funny to see this geekoid trying to look defiant.

Funny, Matt thought, *except for the trouble it would cause.*

"I'm sorry to do it," Saunders said. "But you leave me no choice."

5

That does it, Matt thought glumly. *What are they going to do now?*

The silence of the other make believe sleuths only seemed to underscore his gloom.

Surprisingly, Lucullus Marten provided an answer. His heavy, square face moved to take in the half-circle of unhappy sim participants. Then he turned to Ed Saunders.

"Would you mind very much giving us a moment or two of privacy?" the big man asked.

Saunders looked just like a startled bird. "Um—no," he said. "Take as much time as you need."

An instant later the sim's creator had vanished from his seat.

Marten leaned back in his big thronelike seat. "My dear colleagues," he said. "We face a most onerous accusation—but, it seems, an inescapable one. I was hoping that, in the absence of the teacher, as it were, someone might be willing to admit to a little wrongdoing."

"Just among us?" Maura Slimm said sweetly.

Marten nodded.

But everyone in the room stayed silent.

Marten blew a great, gusty sigh. "I feared it would not be as easy as that," he admitted.

"Of course not!" Milo Krantz snapped. "The . . . hacker"—he made a face as the slang term escaped his lips—"this person would have to be witless to make an admission before witnesses. This is not a case of returning the teacher's apple to the desk, no questions asked. Legal sanctions have been invoked. There may even be criminal penalties."

"Well, that little speech should really encourage whoever it is to speak up," Mick Slimm said tartly.

His wife aimed a suspicious stare at Krantz. "Or maybe you planned it that way to cover yourself. You've obviously been doing a lot of thinking about the situation."

"Again, one would have to be witless *not* to think of the consequences," Krantz snapped in reply.

"Let's just can it," Spike Spanner growled. "We can talk in circles and point fingers until our time is up." He tapped a beefy finger to his chest. "I'm telling you I didn't do it."

"Nor did I," Marten spoke almost immediately.

"Well, I certainly wasn't poking around where I shouldn't." Maura Slimm turned to the man lounging against the arm of her chair. "Were you, Mickey?"

"It strikes me as a sucker's game." Mick Slimm ran a finger along a carefully clipped mustache. "Saunders was only using this case to provide a framework for whatever would happen in our sim. Who'd know which actual facts he might include—and which he would toss out?"

"I suspect our director would have been wiser to let the charade go on," Marten rumbled, "while looking to see whether anyone used any of the discarded elements you mentioned."

"Too late for that," Krantz sniffed. "How unfortunate you didn't mention that plan earlier."

Maura Slimm continued to give the tall man a beady

stare. "What I don't see *you* mentioning is your innocence, Mr. Krantz."

The icy blue eyes behind the spectacles rolled in disgust. "Oh, for heaven's sake! Would you prefer it on a Bible?" He put a hand over his heart. "I swear I am not breaking into secret records on this case." Then Krantz glared round the room. "I trust you're satisfied?"

"I trust nobody," Spike Spanner growled, spearing Matt with a look. "Especially someone who won't take the pledge."

Matt raised a hand. "I swear I didn't hack into anything about the actual case behind the sim. I don't know anything about the Haddings and the Callivants—except what my friend Leif told me."

"Who?" Mick Slimm said.

"The Haddings?" Marten's voice rose. "The *Callivants?*"

Maura Slimm nearly fell off her chair, thrusting an accusing finger at Matt. "You just gave yourself away!" she cried.

Matt hadn't. He'd purposely thrown in the names of the true parties in this mystery, hoping to surprise a response from one of the sleuths. But the ones who weren't exclaiming in surprise had better poker faces than Matt had hoped. He'd thrown away his advantage, with nothing to show for it.

"We know the Peytons in the mystery are a big-shot political family," Spanner said. "That would certainly fit the Callivants, I suppose."

"Hadding—that's the real name of the girl who died?" Krantz sat straighter.

Matt nodded. "None of this came off the Net. I've got a friend who's into society scandal. I picked his brains. The actual case didn't happen in the nineteen thirties, the way Saunders set it up. According to my friend, the case resembles the murder of a girl named Priscilla Hadding, who died back in 1982."

"Eighty-two?" Spanner echoed. "I was still in diapers then. Who'd remember?"

"Somebody starstruck by the social scene," Matt suggested. He shot a silent challenge toward Krantz and the Slimms, all famed as society sleuths. Reluctantly he added Lucullus Marten as well. Most of the big man's cases involved the rich and famous.

"Well, Newman, you shot your bolt," Marten rumbled. "If you hoped to shock anyone into confessing, you've failed. All you've done is make yourself the main suspect."

The whole group settled into mistrustful silence.

At last, Maura Slimm said, "If it was such a big scandal, why isn't it better-known?"

Spike Spanner gave a snort of laughter. "I can answer that one. Hey—look at what happens to anyone who even *mentions* the damned case?"

Megan O'Malley held the door while Leif Anderson stood in the entryway to her house, trying to stamp off the snow sticking to his low boots. They were ankle height, but dressy—the fine leather was already soaked.

"I thought Washington had mild winters. The Brits used to classify their embassy here as subtropical."

"About every fifteen years we get a serious snowstorm." Megan shrugged. "Count your blessings. They're facing a real blizzard up in New York."

"Yeah, but back home, I've got the clothes to deal with this." The snow was gone now, but his shoes squelched as he stamped on the welcome mat.

"Just take 'em off," Megan finally said. "We'll try stuffing them with something and putting them on a heat vent to dry them off." She looked Leif in the eye. "I suppose I should be flattered that you'd brave this weather to come and see me."

"Actually, it's your folks I need to see—or rather, their library."

Now Megan really gave him a look. "I wonder if

you've heard of this wonderful thing called the Net. You can check out whole libraries and even buy books without leaving your house. It beats turning blue at the edges and ruining a pair of shoes."

"I'd rather not advertise what I'm interested in," Leif replied. "But I figure, between your parents' books and yours, you might have some of the stuff here I'm looking for."

"Well, you can ask my folks," Megan said. "They're both home. Some people have enough sense to stay out of the snow."

Megan's mom was a freelancer for *The Washington Post*, while her dad was a mystery author. Both worked out of the house—even if sometimes "work" seemed to mean frowning at the displays of the stories they were writing.

Robert Fitzgerald O'Malley seemed glad for the interruption as the kids came into his office. "Leif!" He exclaimed, turning in surprise. "What brings you out in weather like—whoops!"

His sudden movement dislodged a teetering pile of books on the table next to him. Megan and Leif helped him retrieve the fallen volumes. She wound up holding books titled *The Dictionary of Imaginary Places* and *Modern Metallurgy*. Leif had *True Crimes of the Twentieth Century* and *The Living Sword*. He held the last book up, staring at the cover. "Aldo Nadi's autobiography!"

"That's right," Megan's dad said, "you're a fencer."

"Not in that guy's class." Leif added his books to the new pile Megan was creating on the table. "I can't figure how all this stuff comes together—but then I never expected the way you worked out *Morte Siciliano*, either."

"You read it?" The novelist beamed, almost as proud of his books as he was of his children.

"Leif wants to do a little digging in the library," Megan said.

"Certainly," her father said.

Megan grinned. *Anything for a reader of R. F. O'Malley,* she thought.

"Are you looking for something in particular?" her father asked.

"Biographies, I suppose." Leif pointed to the true crime book in the pile. "And maybe a little of that."

"I got that from Julie. It sounds more like the journalist's side of the stacks." Megan's dad rose from his chair. "Let's go and ask."

Megan generally tried to stay away from her folks while they were working. The little house was noisy enough, thanks to her brothers. Luckily, Mike was off doing research, and Rory, Paul, and Sean were out investigating the exotic phenomenon of snow in D.C.

Julie O'Malley, Megan's mom, had apparently reached a good stopping point in her story when Megan, her dad, and Leif came into the living room. "Biographies?" she said when Dad passed along Leif's request. "Most of them are over here."

"I'm especially looking for anything about the Callivant family," Leif said.

Megan gave him a look. *What was* this *all about? He takes one look at a girl who insults him, and all of a sudden he's digging into her family tree?*

"We've got a couple of books—*Lost Promise,* about Steve, Will, and Martin." Mom made a face. "That was family-authorized, so there are lots of interviews, but it's also something of a puff piece for the Callivants."

She went to the shelf and chose a book. "*America's Anointed* has a lot of stuff about the Callivants, and it's much more balanced. There's a story about Will Callivant's daughter—"

Leif nodded. "The one who got involved in that weird spring break incident with those guys. She's been in a private sanitarium ever since."

Julie O'Malley nodded grimly. "You know that one? While life has been hard on the Callivant men, the family curse seems to be just as hard on the female members of the clan."

Leif dug a piece of paper out of his pocket. "I was wondering if you had *A Death in Haddington*, by Simon Herzen."

Megan stared at the rude noise her mother made. "That piece of . . . writing?" Julie O'Malley shook her head. "I was in journalism school when that came out. The buzz about the book was tremendous. Everyone said Si Herzen was going to blow the top off a big cover-up."

Leif leaned forward eagerly. "And?"

"Then it hit the stands and sank without a trace. I read it. Herzen had done a clip job, more or less cutting and pasting what the media had printed and broadcast about the Hadding case. The book stank, but we never knew why. Maybe the publisher's lawyers got into the act, or the Callivants got to Herzen or the publishing company." Megan's mom looked disgusted. "I wouldn't give that book house room."

The library shelves did yield a few other volumes about the Callivants. A couple were pretty old. One had a couple of chapters on Priscilla Hadding's death.

Leif thanked Megan's mom. Then Megan led him into the kitchen to get some plastic bags to wrap up the books.

As soon as they were alone, Megan folded her arms and stood in Leif's path. "You're up to something. What's all this about the Callivants?"

"It's for Matt," Leif said. "He's in trouble, and the Callivants may be the cause of it."

Megan listened to the story of how Matt's mystery sim had spiraled out of control. "I guess we should be glad we didn't get into this world to play," she finally said. "What's he going to do?"

Leif shrugged. "Right now he's just watching the clock tick away."

While Megan worked to make a good, waterproof package, her mother came back in. "Here are your shoes,

Leif, but I think you'd be better off with a pair of Rory's boots."

She looked worriedly out of the kitchen window. "The snow has stopped, but now we're getting freezing rain." A car went skidding by on the street. "Snow's bad enough in this town, but this may even be worse."

Matt hadn't even gone out of his house. He'd sat in the kitchen, explaining things to his parents . . . and watching the clock move ever closer to Ed Saunders's deadline. How long would it take the Callivants' lawyers to start badgering him and his parents?

Matt's father was obviously thinking the same thing—and worrying about it. "I just don't understand," he said for what had to be the fiftieth time. "How could you sign an agreement like that?"

"It's fairly standard, Dad. Don't you read the fine print whenever you load in a new program?" Matt said gloomily. "It's just never been an issue in any of the programs I've used."

"I find it hard to believe that giving away those kinds of rights would be standard," Gordon Hunter said.

Matt's mom called to them from the living room. They came in to find her standing in front of the computer console. Some sort of document, much enlarged, floated before her in holographic display. "I've been calling up the agreements for various sims we've used," she said. "Look here."

"That's my tennis game," Matt's father said, looking at the heading of the display.

"Read this bit of fine print."

Word for word, it was the same as the clause in the agreement Matt had signed, giving the sim operator the right, if necessary, to reveal the identities of all participants.

Gordon was shocked. "I thought the Revised Privacy Act of 2013 was supposed to protect consumers against things like this."

"And I suppose this little clause is what the lawyers came up with to get around that law," Marissa Hunter said grimly. "It's also in my flight simulator. As Matt says, it appears to be an industry standard."

"I'll bet we could challenge that in court," Matt's father said.

His wife merely gave him a look.

Sure, we could challenge it, Matt thought. *If we had money like Leif's father, we could even afford the time and the lawyers.* But Dad was a teacher, and Mom a career Navy officer. Their income wouldn't let them hire a fraction of the kind of legal talent the Callivants already had working on this.

Dad must have realized the same thing even as the words were coming out of his mouth. Silently he led the way back to the kitchen to watch the hands of the clock advance.

The deadline came, then dinnertime. Everybody in the Hunter family barely touched the food on their plates, waiting for . . . something. A call, a virtmail message—Matt had ordered his program to sound a special chime if anything came in.

There was only silence as they tried to eat, silence as they cleared the table, silence as they cleaned the dishes.

"You would think Saunders would let us know, one way or the other," Matt complained as he stacked plates in the kitchen cabinet. "Unless it might have something to do with the weather?"

Marissa Hunter gave her son a wry smile. "They don't usually declare snow days for legal problems," she said.

Matt waited a little while longer, then finally said, "I'm going to call him."

Going to the living room console, he recited the Net address that had engraved itself into his memory. The computer display blinked for a moment, then Ed Saunders appeared. "Can't talk to you right now," his image announced. "But you can leave a detailed visual or virtmail message—your choice."

Disgusted, Matt cut the connection. "He's not there! What would he be doing out on a night like this?"

"He could be hiding behind his automated answering system," Matt's father suggested, "using it to screen his calls."

"You mean he doesn't have the nerve to face us." Matt angrily returned to the computer, giving it a new set of orders. The machine took a moment or two to sift through the Net. But it finally came up with a physical address to match the owner of the Net site.

Matt told the computer to plot the location on a map of D.C., marking the nearest Metro stations.

"What are you thinking of, Matthew?" his father asked, his voice concerned.

"I want to know where we stand with this mess," Matt replied. "It looks as though Saunders lives only a couple of blocks from the Waterfront Metro station."

"You're not thinking of going out in this ice storm," his mother said.

"I'm thinking of going *under* it." Matt looked at his parents. "Do we really just want to sit here and wait for whatever it is to fall on us?"

In the end Matt and his father, bundled up like Eskimos, wound up setting off for Ed Saunders's house. Several times on the long, slippery walk to the Metro station, Matt wished he hadn't been so persuasive. The frozen rain was coming down in tiny pellets of ice, which flew along on a howling wind. And no matter which direction they walked in, the wind seemed to be gusting right into their faces.

Now I know how it feels to be sandblasted, Matt thought as a new crop of sleet tore across his exposed skin. He could barely see where he was going through his slitted eyes, and every step he took along the slick sidewalk threatened to dump him on his butt.

It was a distinct relief to skid down the stairs to the station. But then they faced an infuriating wait for a train. "A good part of the Metro system is open to the sky,"

Dad said. "I guess even the rails are getting iced up."

At last their train arrived and took them, along with a few other harassed-looking evening commuters, across town. Clinging to an ice-crusted handrail, they made their way up the stairs. Of course, the wind had swung around again so that it was in their faces.

Head down, his cheeks feeling as if they were being peppered with tiny buckshot, Matt half-walked, half-skated through deserted streets.

Sure, he thought. *Anybody with an ounce of brains in their heads would stay indoors and warm during a storm like this.*

He and his dad slogged along until Gordon Hunter asked, "Two blocks, you said. How many blocks have we gone now?"

Holding on to a glazed light pole, Matt swung around to squint up at the street sign. Great. Now only half his face was being ice-blasted. "It's right around the—"

He broke off as he spotted the lump in the middle of the block off to their left, almost beyond the wan circle of light thrown by the ice-frosted streetlight. It was a human-shaped lump, half-on, half-off the sidewalk.

"Dad!" Matt burst out, skidding toward the still form.

When he got close enough to make out details, Matt stopped so quickly, his father almost rammed into him from behind.

The ice-crusted lump *was* human. Worse, it was familiar.

Ed Saunders's bluish face stared blankly up into the pelting ice storm, immobile despite the stinging particles rattling down on his cheeks, his nose . . . his open eyes.

Matt didn't need to see the reddish-black stain on the curb beneath Saunders's head to know that the man wouldn't feel anything ever again.

6

After nearly having his face peeled off by gusts of wind-borne ice, Matt was glad for the shelter of the police patrol car. He'd had to open his coat to get out his wallet-phone and call for help. For the rest of the time he and his father had stood at the scene of the accident, Matt hadn't been able to shake the resulting chill.

Maybe it was psychological, a reaction to standing beside a dead body. There was no doubt that Ed Saunders was dead. Matt had tried to resuscitate him, but it was like working with a very stiff dummy. He knew it was hopeless, but he'd had to try. Saunders's cold flesh had just sucked away more of Matt's body heat. Worst of all was the knowledge that the effort was a lost cause. Saunders already had a thin coating of ice over his eyeballs.

All in all, Matt had been glad when the police officers had arrived and put him in the stuffy warmth of their squad car. But the smell was wearing on him now. It stank of harsh cleanser and, under that, just the barest trace of vomit. Matt gulped against a suddenly rebellious stomach, wishing he hadn't recognized that other scent.

He tried to distract himself by thinking of what lay ahead. His dad wasn't with him. Gordon Hunter was sitting in the sector sergeant's car, which had arrived just a moment after the ambulance Matt had called. But the paramedics had stayed in the meat wagon while the cops stood hunched in their blue parkas, guarding the scene of the accident—or, perhaps, of the crime.

It looked to Matt as if Saunders had slipped on the ice and cracked his head on the curb. But as he sat in the caged rear of the patrol car, he had to admit the possibility that Saunders might have had his head cracked before he hit the ground. No wonder the cops had been so interested in the people who had found the body and called in the accident. That's why they'd separated him from his father—so neither would hear the other's story.

So, what would Monty Newman have done in this situation? There was at least one Lucullus Marten novel where the assistant sleuth had been accused of murder. . . .

Annoyingly, Matt's thoughts refused to get together and stay together. His eyes kept closing. The warm air wafting from the car's heater was putting him to sleep.

The blast of cold air and ice that invaded the car when the door opened was a shock. But Matt got an even bigger shock when he managed to focus his eyes. He knew the man leaning into the car. It was David Gray's father.

Martin Gray was a detective for the D.C. police—on the homicide squad. He looked almost as surprised to see Matt as Matt was to see him. "You're a long way from home—on a night when most people would prefer to stay there," David's dad said.

Matt replied with a bone-cracking yawn. "Sorry," he apologized. "I was dozing off in here." He blinked. "My father and I were going to see Ed Saunders, the—the man out there." Matt pointed through the fogged window toward the curbside.

"It must have been pretty important to come out in the middle of a storm," Martin Gray prompted.

"Seemed so at the time," Matt said. "I'd better start at the beginning." He told the detective about the sim and the resulting problems. "Is there some reason to think that Saunders was killed?" he asked when he'd finished.

"I wouldn't exactly call you a suspect," Martin Gray replied dryly. "But what you tell me does explain something we found on the late Mr. Saunders." He held up a piece of paper. "I guess you didn't notice this in his pocket."

Matt shuddered. "I was just trying to give him CPR." An unpleasant memory intruded—how Saunders's ice-impregnated coat had crackled under his hands while Matt tried to revive him.

"Saunders must have been working on an answer for those lawyers you mentioned." Detective Gray held out the paper. It was a computer printout, but somebody had attacked the crisp letters with a smeary ballpoint pen. Lots of words had been scribbled over, with whole new sections of the letter put in by hand. "Is that the name of the law firm? Do you recognize any of the names in the list down here?"

Matt looked over out the top of the letter for the address and name of the law firm, and got a quick glimpse of the list of what he guessed were Ed's sim users before Martin Gray covered the addresses. A line of names ran down the left in the body of the letter, with addresses on the right. "That's the firm," he said. "As I told you before, I don't know the real names of the sim users, only the names of the characters they were playing."

Even as he spoke, though, Matt was frantically trying to memorize those real names now. He only caught one name and address, and another name from the next line.

T. Flannery he thought, trying to memorize the next part. *2545 Decatur Place.* The next name was K. Jones, and that was all that Matt's sleep-deprived and shock-dulled brain managed to hold on to. He repeated them silently until they seemed to be echoing in his head. "You think one of these people did . . . that?" Matt gestured again out the window. More police had arrived, taking pictures and checking the area. Now they stepped back to let the paramedics slip Ed Saunders into a body bag.

"I don't know. To tell you the truth, I wouldn't necessarily be here, except that the sector sergeant is a friend of mine . . . and I happened to be in the neighborhood." Detective Gray shrugged. "Whenever anybody who's not directly under a doctor's care passes away, the case is treated as a possibly suspicious death."

Matt shook his head. "Boy, I thought school was tough—but if you need a doctor's note for *this!*"

His half-punchy comment got a laugh out of Martin Gray. Then the expression on the police officer's face sobered.

"Yeah, well," David's dad said. "On the other hand, Mr. Saunders isn't really going to care about it, now . . . is he?"

Leif was lying in bed, surrounded by books about the Callivants, when the chimes announcing an incoming call began to ring. He swung both feet to the floor and activated his bedroom console. A second later a holo image swam into view—a very pink-faced Matt Hunter. Before he could speak, Leif erupted in a thunderous sneeze.

"I guess I wasn't the only one who was out in the weather," Matt said, massaging his cheeks. "I still can't quite feel my face."

"Sounds charming," Leif sneezed again and scrabbled for a tissue to wipe his runny nose.

"Not as charming as what you've got," Matt shot back with a grin. "You don't look your usual suave self."

Leif looked down at the old sweatsuit he was using as pajamas, his nose wrinkling from the pungent scent of the herbal rub his mother had insisted on slathering over his chest. "Just be glad you can't smell me." He looked keenly at his friend. "What sent you out into the howling blizzard? Is it something to do with your problems?"

Matt nodded. "I've got a new one now. Ed Saunders is dead and the cops are investigating."

Leif stopped dabbing at his nose. "You think one of your playmates resented this deadline of his that much?"

"Who knows? As far as I can tell, he didn't let us know how things had turned out. When I tried to call, I got his automatic message system. Dad and I finally took the Metro, hoping to talk this out face-to-face. We were half a block from his address when we found him—literally in the gutter."

"What happened? Murder most foul? Hit-and-run? A falling icicle?" Leif was downright disappointed when he heard that Saunders had most likely been the victim of a fatal slip on the icy sidewalk.

"David's dad has no sense of drama," Leif complained.

"I'm sure that's the last thing he wants in his job," Matt agreed. When he went on to describe the letter and the attached list, Leif's interest quickened.

"The List of Ed Saunders," he said in a throbbing voice. "No, it's not going to work as a title. *"The List of Edward Saunders.* Or maybe *The Curious Case of Edward Saunders."*

"Be hard to top the book you've got in your hand," Matt replied. "What is that? *Political Crimes and Misdemeanors?"*

Leif held up the book he'd brought along with him. "Just something I borrowed from Mrs. O'Malley," he said. "It's got some stuff about the death in Haddington."

"That's the last thing I have to worry about," Matt said. "Right now I have to see how this death in Washington affects what's going on with the Callivant lawyers." Matt hesitated for a second. "I got a look at that list you were kidding about."

"Really? I don't suppose there was anybody you recognized." Leif grinned. "I always figured Maj Greene for a secret Lucullus Marten fan."

Matt shook his head. "No friends, no enemies, no obvious murderers. Just a bunch of unknown names."

Leif looked expectantly at his friend's image. "So did you copy them all down? We could check them out."

"I got one name and address, and one more name." He looked embarrassed.

"That's it?" Leif asked.

"Hey, I'd just struggled through a storm with a lawsuit hanging over my head, I found a body and gave CPR to a cold corpse, and when I was just about frozen stiff, then I was put as a possible homicide suspect into a police car with the heater doing overtime. I had just about zonked off when David's dad started talking to me."

"At least you got two out of five."

Matt scowled. "More like one out of five. Do you know how many K. Joneses there are in this city?"

Leif laughed, then coughed. "Not to mention the surrounding suburban counties. I take it that's the name that didn't have the address?"

Matt nodded. "The other is T. Flannery." He reeled off the rest of the address.

"Decatur Place?" Leif closed his eyes, calling up a mental map. "That's a street up by Dupont Circle. Pretty nice address." The area was in Northwest Washington, where developers now waged a continual war with people who wanted to preserve the old buildings in the neighborhood. "Have you checked it out?"

"There's no listing for a T. Flannery at that address," Matt replied.

"And why would anybody give an unlisted connection, even for a noncommercial test sim like Saunders was running?" Leif felt his lips twitch into a smile. "I begin to see why you decided to call me."

Still maintaining his connection with Matt, Leif warmed up his computer and began giving some orders. Besides communications codes, he had access to a wider range of trace programs and databases—some of them even legal—than Matt did.

"The city directory doesn't show a T. Flannery living at that address," Leif announced, looking at the print display now floating beside the image of Matt's head. "No rent records, or condo mortgages. But I've got clear indications of electrical bills, water bills, and sewage lines going to the property. It's not empty land. So who owns that chunk of D.C.?"

A second later, and he was taking in the results of his search, frowning.

"What is it?" Matt said, leaning forward as if he could peer around Leif and see whatever he was reading.

"The owner of the property at 2545 Decatur is the Roman Catholic Diocese of Washington. It's St. Adelbert's Church." Leif glanced at his friend. "Which means you either misread the list—or T. Flannery is using a fake address."

"The list was printed out," Matt said. "That address was probably the only part of the letter that hadn't been scratched over and edited." He thought for a moment, then shook his head decisively. "I don't think I messed it up."

"Then we have somebody hiding behind a church. Somebody—" Leif's triumphant speech was interrupted by another sneeze.

"Gesundheit," Matt said. "I'm glad I'm only here in holoform. I'd hate to catch what you're spreading."

"Thanks for all the sympathy," Leif said with considerable irony. "We're looking here at somebody who would maybe make a reasonable suspect for prying around in sealed records," Leif pressed on, then went for broke. "Somebody who might even have a reason to shut Saunders up—permanently."

"Oh, please!" Matt burst out. "That was an accident. Tomorrow's news reports are going to be full of the statistics from this storm. X number of inches of snow. X number of car accidents. So many people injured by mishaps on the ice."

"And so many dead." Leif tilted his head, a look of grudging admiration on his face. "If you wanted to get rid of somebody, it would be a perfect time."

"Even David's father hinted that he didn't see anything more than an accident—and he's a homicide detective." Matt crossed his arms, the man with the proof.

"A homicide detective called to a scene where usually you get a couple of patrol cops, the local sergeant, and somebody from the medical examiner's office. That's the way they do it in New York." An elderly neighbor of the Andersons had abruptly dropped dead in their condominium lobby. Although she was wealthy—anybody who lived at that address would have to be—that was as far as the NYPD went on a case of doubtful death.

Matt, however, wasn't really listening. He was still wrestling with the problem of another address. "Could this T. Flannery be homeless?" he suggested. "I know the problem's a lot better than it used to be, but it's not completely fixed. I know that churches sometimes offer the homeless a place to stay."

"And, of course, access to their computer systems, so the homeless folk can play detective games," Leif added, shaking his head. "It doesn't add up, Matt."

He turned back to his computer. "Well, there's one way we can find out." He asked for the communications code for St. Adelbert's Roman Catholic Church, then told his system to connect with that number.

A second later the image of a young man in a sport shirt appeared beside Matt. The guy was sitting behind a office desk, holding some papers. "St. Adelbert's Church," he said pleasantly.

"I'm trying to get hold of a T. Flannery, and this was the number I was given," Leif responded.

The young man on the other end of the connection smiled apologetically. "I'm afraid Father Tim is at the hospital right now. All those accidents this evening. Is it something about the youth ministry? I could help you with that. Or would you like to leave a message?"

"A message for Father Tim. Yes, maybe that's the best way." Leif fought to control the grin tugging at his lips. He gave his name and communications code. "Tell him it's about a mystery—a sorrowful mystery."

7

Matt was actually sitting in Leif's room—as he said to Leif, getting in a little face time despite the risk of infection—when Father Flannery called back. At the first sound of his voice Matt knew immediately who he played in the sim.

The priest was younger than his counterpart. He had the same pinkish coloring as Spike Spanner, but was much slimmer, with a head of wavy reddish-brown hair. His eyes were much milder than the two-fisted P.I. he portrayed. But they sharpened when they focused on Matt. "Mr. Anderson, I presume?"

"A reasonable assumption," Leif said, "considering that you saw him unmasked at Mr. Saunders's virtual office. But I'm Leif Anderson, and I'm just an interested bystander in the situation. My friend is Matt Hunter."

"Young man, are you sure you aren't a party to our sim? You don't look like Lucullus Marten, but you certainly managed to sound like him right then," the priest said suspiciously. "You also sound like this note I just got via virtmail."

He held up a printout of the same message that had sent Matt out into the cold to confer with his friend. It was simple enough:

Should you appear at the address below at seven P.M. this evening, you will learn something to your advantage.

Beneath that were the coordinates for a Net site. No letterhead, no return address, and as far as the boys had been able to trace it back, the message had apparently bounced at random through the international webwork of computers for hours without ever initiating from anywhere.

"I got one of those, too," Matt said.

"The wording sounds like something a golden age detective would use in a newspaper ad looking for a witness." Father Flannery still regarded them suspiciously. "I could see it coming from Lucullus Marten."

"Or from Milo Krantz," Matt replied.

"Let's face it. Notes like that go back to Sherlock Holmes. We have to expect that whoever is playing the characters in this sim would know about that tradition." Leif nodded politely. "Including you, Father."

"I can assure you I had nothing to do with the illegal computer entries which started this trouble," Father Flannery said stiffly. "I'm willing to open my computer for an audit to prove my statements."

Matt looked at Leif, who looked away. Not many people would allow their private files to be pawed open by strangers.

"I'm inclined to accept Father Flannery's word," Matt said.

"Then we know the true identities of two of the six players in Ed Saunders's sim," Leif said. "Matt, I know you're too much of a straight arrow to go hacking in government files, or even in Mr. Saunders's computer. Somebody, most likely the original hacker, must have raided Saunders's files. That would be child's play, if what Sauders told us is correct, compared to some of the official record storehouses that were cracked before the sim was shut down and this whole mess started. Saunders's computer is the most likely source of the address list for your virtmail messages. And I'd bet that most, if not all, of the participants in the sim got the same message."

Father Tim nodded, obviously following Leif's logic. "But I would guess you're innocent of sending the message, because you called me and left your number before I received the message. Why go through such an elaborate rigamarole when you'd already contacted me directly?" He still didn't look friendly or happy. "That only leaves the question of how you got my real identity and address when you've only seen me in proxy form in the sim."

"Father Tim, I don't know if you've heard this, but Ed Saunders is dead. My father and I were the ones who discovered the body," Matt said. "I had discussed the problem of the potential lawsuit with my parents, and when the deadline passed with no word, we went out into some nasty weather for a little face-to-face." He shuddered. "But we were too late to talk with him."

"A horrible accident," Father Tim said gently. "I read about it in *The Washington Post*."

"While they were questioning me, the police showed me the hard copy of a letter Ed had been drafting to answer the lawyers," Matt went on. "I managed to see two names and one address. Yours."

"Lucky me," the priest said. Then he laughed and shrugged. "Two out of six. Monty Newman would say that was good baseball, but poor detecting."

Leif chuckled. "Spike Spanner might get away with a crack like that, too." He paused. "How did you wind up choosing a rough diamond like the Spikester, Father Flannery?"

"I discovered the Spikester, as you call him, in an old

flatfilm television series in the last century." The priest shrugged. "I became a fan. Over the years I tracked down all the episodes and the various films and books."

"Wasn't there also a Spike Spanner holo series a little while back?" Matt asked.

Father Flannery made a disgusted noise. "It had a former male model prancing around in it, trying to convince people that he was tough. The old versions were much better." Then he shrugged and grinned. "Still, I decided that if a silly male model could do it, why couldn't I?"

Leif chuckled. "Spanner isn't exactly a 'turn the other cheek' kind of guy."

"More like a 'kick rump before somebody tries to kick thine,' " the priest said with a laugh. "Playing the character helped me vent off some of the frustration of my job, I admit. Some of my friends from the seminary play sports to do the same thing."

"So your superiors would have no problem with what you were doing?" Leif pressed.

"About what I do for entertainment, no," Father Flannery's face darkened. "About being accused of illegally hacking into secure government databases to win a sim mystery—now that would bring up lots of problems."

Matt pointed to the printout still in Flannery's hand. "Will I see you—or rather, Spike—at seven o'clock?"

Father Flannery nodded unhappily. "I'm curious enough, or desperate enough, to go. Although I'd prefer to know who my host was."

"If I were you, I'd like to know who the whole cast of characters was, while I was at it." Leif's eyes got a faraway look. "Maybe I'll take a whack at that myself."

For someone actually traveling its electronic pathways, the Net could be a neon kaleidoscope, an ever-shifting cityscape whose vibrant colors glared against a blacker-than-black backdrop.

Leif had decided to take a crack at the offer he'd made while Matt was visiting. He waited until Matt left, shortly after Father Flannery had cut his Net connection. Matt was a little annoyed, since Leif wouldn't discuss how he intended to expose the identities of the mystery role-players. But Leif figured some things were easier if you didn't know all the details. That was especially true of Mr. Straight-Arrow Matt Hunter, who'd told Martin Gray and his father about the anonymous message before heading over to tell Leif. Not that the cops were likely to tell Matt what—if anything—they planned to do with the information. Or whether they'd in fact decide to take action. Matt said that Mr. Gray hadn't been too interested—it seemed that the police were leaning very strongly toward accidental death rather than homicide in the case of Ed Saunders. No, Leif figured, if he and Matt wanted a real answer to the mystery, they'd have to find it themselves.

As soon as Matt was out the door, Leif warmed up his computer. The person he wanted to contact was not at the last address Leif had for him, so he had a little searching to do.

Finally Leif got what he wanted, sat in his computer-link couch, closed his eyes, and gave the order. After a moment of nasty mental static, he was flying through the Day-Glo buildings of the Net. His hurtling course took him to a relatively quiet section of the garish metropolis, far from the fanciful sites of the big corporate players. His destination was in one of the much simpler, almost boxlike virtual constructions that offered a Net presence for smaller businesses.

A glance at the target building's directory showed an importer of skimpy Brazilian beachwear (complete with picture), a genealogist, and a craftsman devoted to repairing mechanical wristwatches.

Talk about your obsolete technologies, Leif thought. *What's next? A blacksmith in the basement?*

Some of the listings gave only a vague company title or someone's name. The suite Leif was headed for—1019—had only a blank space showing.

Leif hurtled up to the tenth level and went down an anonymous hallway past door after identical glowing door. The entrance to suite 1019 was unlocked. No security worries here. Uninvited intruders would just have to suffer the consequences to their computer files, their systems, and—knowing the guy behind this front— maybe to their health.

Taking a deep virtual breath, Leif moved in. The place was Spartan—an empty space that would have echoed in real life. Walls, ceiling, and floor were bare. Leif saw a single desk, equipped with what looked like a turn-of-the-century computer system. A flatscreen monitor glowed over the box of the central processing unit. In front lay an old-fashioned keyboard.

As Leif came closer, the screen suddenly lit up.

Letters appeared on the glowing display. *Long time no see.*

"Do I have to type in a reply?" Leif asked the empty air.

We hear all, even if we don't necessarily know all, the screen flashed back.

Leif shook his head. This particular hacker was never easy to get a hold of. He changed his virtual address often. In fact, he moved so often that Leif wondered if he really paid for his office space. And he (at least, Leif thought it was a he) never dealt face-to-face with his clients. Communication was always arranged though some sort of weird cutout. Once, Leif had entered a door like the one he'd just gone through and found a perfect replica of a starship bridge from an old sci-fi show. A silvery female voice had answered him then.

So what's the problem at hand? the unknown hacker asked. *I already said we don't know all.*

"I have a friend who's going to be meeting some people tonight," Leif said. "He doesn't know them, and they'll be all proxied up. What he needs is a tracer to find out who they really are."

I hope your "friend" has a fat credit line, the hacker's response blinked onto the screen.

"I'll freight it—within limits," Leif hastily added. "Is it a technical problem, or just a question of speed?"

After prompting Leif for the time and location of this meeting—and getting his answer—the computer screen was blank for a while. *Six hours from now—not optimal. But it may be possible to adapt an already existing product.*

The next few exchanges broke down to the sort of haggling done eight thousand years before computers existed. After taking a bigger hit in his credit account than he liked—but contingent on timely delivery—Leif got ready to leave.

But the computer wasn't done with him. *The existing program requires contact with the virtual form of the people to be traced.* The monitor blinked at him. *Any suggestions as to a delivery vector?*

Leif began to grin. "As a matter of fact, I can suggest one," he said.

As Matt came to his destination, the Net's usual brilliant colors faded to the dimmest of outlines. Not surprising. Out here in the middle of virtual nowhere, there was no need for advertising, no need to catch the eye. Not enough eyes came through here to be caught. Below him, a faint white glow delineated a vista of featureless black boxes. They stretched, row after row, to the virtual horizon, like chips on a monstrous circuit board—or more poetically, like mausoleums in a cemetery.

This is where information went to die. Officially it was known as long-term filing, but most people called it dead storage.

Matt had suspected this was where he'd be heading, even before he and Leif had decoded the address on the virtmail invitation. Each of these mammoth boxes represented an archive of government or corporate records, stuff that wasn't needed except maybe once in a blue moon. The data was supposed to lie here, safe and quiet, in the unlikely eventuality that someone would want to look at it again.

However, hackers sometimes worked their way into these boxes, deleting the data and using the space for programs of their own, virtual meeting rooms, sometimes even illegal sims.

I suppose that's okay if they're eliminating what people owe in library fines from 2013, Matt thought. *But what if somebody has to prove military service from twenty years ago, or that they filed the correct forms on a claim way back when?*

He throttled back the spurt of anger he always felt when people fracked around where they shouldn't have. In a bizarre way, this obviously clandestine meeting place was reassuring. Since the message arrived, he'd had the niggling fear that this was actually a setup by the Callivant lawyers. But this *felt* like a hacker's work—an amateur hacker pushed to the limit.

Matt finally arrived at a big, dim box, apparently no different from the ones on either side of it. But this was the address on the virtmail invitation. *Let's hope whoever sent it doesn't suffer from typos,* Matt told himself as he went inside.

This was the place. The interior had been programmed into a shadowy warehouse. *Which,* Matt suddenly thought, *is really what these places are.* But it was also just the sort of meeting place a fan of 1930s mysteries would create. The echoing space was almost pitch-black, with a few pools of light from single bulbs in tin shades like flattened cones.

You could hide an army out in the darkness, but Matt figured there were only five other people out there. He could even hear them breathing. Problem was, nobody wanted to announce him- or herself, because the others would then think that person had called the meeting. And then that person would be accused as the hacker who'd gotten the names for this meeting—and probably gotten everyone into trouble in the first place.

Looks like it's amateur night all around, Matt thought. *Lucky thing I talked this over with Leif and Martin Gray.*

Matt reached into the satchel dangling from his shoulder and drew out a flashlight. Switching it on, he speared the blackness with a fan of brilliance. "Anybody here?" he called.

The flash immediately caught two figures—the Slimms. "See, Mick?" Maura said to her husband. "I told you we should have brought one of those."

Now that Matt had initiated things, Marten, Krantz, and Spanner also stepped into the light.

"I won't express any surprise that we're all here," Marten said, leaning his weight on his cane. "Certainly, I didn't hesitate to clear my desk and plan to come when I got an anonymous invitation this morning. Self-protection is a strong incentive for appearing."

"You mean from the lawyers?" Krantz asked.

"I mean protection of our lives," Marten replied. "The circumstances of Mr. Saunders's death—"

"Oh, come on!" Matt burst out. "He slipped on the ice in front of his house and cracked his skull. I was there—and how do you know so much about it?"

Marten glared at him. "I have my methods. I'm sure we are all sufficiently aware of cases where cracked skulls were not the result of falls, but rather, the cause. We must consider the probability that the recent storm merely offered a convenient opportunity for someone to conceal a murder."

"M-murder?" Maura Slimm echoed in an uneasy voice.

Mick Slimm took her arm. "All right, Marten, or whoever you are. Sure, we're aware of cases like you've described—but most, if not all, took place in books . . . as fiction."

"You offer Saunders's murder as a probability,"

Krantz horned in. "Shouldn't you say 'possibility?' According to what I've found out, even the police think it was probably an accident."

"And when will the probability of accident shift into the possibility of murder?" Marten demanded. "When another of us suffers an unexpected 'accident'? Or a third?"

"You're raving. We're all here, aren't we? I think you are borrowing trouble here—and we have enough trouble with just the lawyers going after Ed's sim. So what do you want to do?" Spike Spanner looked uncomfortable. Or rather, Matt suspected, Father Flannery was wrestling with some unpleasant prospects. "Do you intend to go to the cops and rile them up about a possible murder case? Who are you going to give them as a suspect?"

"Those lawyers who were badgering him?" Maura Slimm offered hopefully.

Milo Krantz gave Marten a squinty-eyed look. "Or do you propose to give them one of us, killing to keep the lawyers away?"

Matt said nothing, aware that the police were aware of the game-players and this motive. Detective Martin Gray wasn't questioning anyone because the case was still officially an accident, and would remain so unless the medical examiner found some evidence to the contrary.

In holo-dramas, the coroner's report always seemed ready within minutes of the victim's death. From what David and his father had to say, however, even speedy results took days.

"What I propose," Marten said, "is a defensive alliance. Each of us needs someone to guard our backs. As it stands now, if one of us is threatened, how will the others know?"

Krantz got icy. "You expect us to reveal our true identities?"

"Of course. How else would we know of further 'accidents'?" Marten leaned his bulk forward. "I will reveal myself, but not unilaterally. It must be all or nothing."

"You know, for somebody who claims he was just invited here this morning, you've wound up running the meeting," Spanner said suspiciously.

"Right." Mick Slimm gave Marten a long stare. "All or nothing means one person can veto the deal. Since the hacker already knows our names, that person benefits if everybody else remains suspicious—and ignorant. What better way to drive a wedge between us all than to try stampeding us into dropping our masks immediately?"

Marten glared at him. "What better way to invite suspicion than to vote against my idea?"

"This is the part I hate in every mystery story!" Maura burst out. "The bad guy knows that we can only guess who he is. But we know that he knows, or at least we guess that he knows, or he guesses that we're guessing—"

"Bah, madam," Marten interrupted, "what you're doing is called attempting a deduction without facts." He looked around at the other sleuths. "If all agree to my suggestion, we'll have a few facts to work with. If only one person objects, that becomes a fact in itself."

"I think two people are going to object," Mick Slimm said. "Maura and I know each other in real life. We can guard each other's backs."

"It may be all over, now that Saunders is—" Maura broke off. "We don't even know he sent anything to those lawyers."

"You don't think that law firm could get access to the late Mr. Saunders' computer?" Marten rumbled. "The police certainly could."

"Only if they think there was a crime involved," Milo Krantz coolly pointed out. "From the news reports, it's being treated as an accident. As the situation stands, one irresponsible hacker has our identities. Your plan opens the possibility of other irresponsible parties using that information. I fear I'd have to reject that."

"Thanks for the vote of confidence," Spanner growled.

Marten merely nodded—a tiny shift of his great head.

"Just for the record, what is your opinion, Mr. Spanner? Mr. Newman?"

"I never thought I'd say it, but I'm with the big man," Spanner said. "All, or nothing at all."

Matt shrugged. "You all saw me without my mask on, but I'm not giving out a name and address without getting everyone else's in return." He reached into his satchel again. "But there's no reason for everybody to go away mad. I'm betting that whoever brought us here will arrange for regular meetings. Call it the sleuth's club."

He came out with a bottle of champagne and some glasses. "What do you say? If we can't have an alliance, let's go for friendly suspicion."

Matt sat the glasses from his satchel down and popped the cork on the bottle. Champagne gushed out to spatter on Marten's shoes.

"*Must* you act like a jackass, Monty?" the big man angrily demanded.

"Sorry, boss," Matt said with a grin. "Care for a bit of the bubbly?"

"You know my preferences," Marten snapped. "I don't like the stuff."

Matt shrugged. "I know hard cider is your drink of choice, but I figured I'd be just about as successful at convincing you to try it as you were with your proposal."

The Slimms each took a glass. So did a squinty-eyed Spike Spanner. He also handed one to Krantz, who shook his head. "I, too, must decline. It reduces the faculties."

"Don't be a party poo—whoops!" The glass Spanner held out tipped, dribbling champagne down the front of the man-about-town's exquisite vest.

Krantz whipped the fluted handkerchief from the breast pocket of his jacket, dabbing at the stain. "Another reason why I don't care to indulge. And you've barely had a sip!"

Matt touched the glass to his lips. The bubbles really did come up to tickle his nose. And it tasted rank to him. Leif claimed that the bottle was programmed to taste like the very best stuff. Matt didn't care. The champagne was only the delivery vector. Everybody whose identity they didn't know had been marked.

Marten had to know his suggestion was doomed from the start, Matt thought. *Krantz called it. Not one of the folks behind these proxies wants irresponsible people, maybe even litigious or murderous people, knowing who they really are.*

Raising his glass in a mock toast, he gave the other sleuths a Monty Newman grin. *Too bad that's just what's going to happen.*

8

"Glad to see you got over your cold," Megan told Leif as she held open the door to her house. He came in balancing a stack of books, topped by her brother's boots.

"I used the sick time to get what I needed out of these." He carefully deposited the pile on a kitchen chair. "If your parents are in, I'd like to thank them for letting me borrow all this stuff."

"Sure," Megan said. "After we check the books."

"Check?" Leif echoed. "For what?"

"That you haven't cut out any of Nikki Callivant's pictures," Megan informed him sweetly. "That's how I understand this obsession with public—or semipublic figures—begins. Clipped pictures pasted up on walls. Little shrines built in the corner of a room. And the next thing we know, Nikki Callivant is bringing in the police to arrest another stalker." She shook her head. "I don't want to see you going that route, Anderson. For one thing, I am not going on HoloNews to say, 'He was a quiet boy. I can't believe he'd do anything like that.' "

"But I'd never—"

She gave him a 200-watt glare. "I wouldn't put anything past you—the dumber, the better."

Leif rolled his eyes. "Thanks for your concern, but I don't have any personal interest in Nikki Callivant. This is just research to help out Matt."

"If he's in trouble with the Callivants, he's going to need more than just research to save him," Megan said.

"I've already been working on that—which is more than you can say."

Megan shrugged. "He hasn't asked *me*."

She grinned as Leif struggled not to snap back at her. Instead, he changed the subject. "I suppose you've heard how Matt found the guy who was running the sim."

"Yeah." Megan shuddered. "Pretty gross."

"You may not have heard about the threats this Saunders guy made before he died or about the letter he was carrying." He went on to explain about the list of sim participants, and how they'd found Father Flannery.

"Somebody—probably the hacker who started all the problems—called a meeting of the wannabe detectives. I managed to get my hands on a tracking program, and Matt used it to trace the people's proxies back through the Net."

"Just happened to get your hands on that, did you?" Megan mocked.

Leif's ears reddened. "It was only a little trouble, and it helped out a friend. Matt called me just as I was leaving to make this delivery. He and the priest are going to spend the afternoon paying a few real-world visits to the participants in the sim."

Megan whistled. "That should be interesting."

"Especially since one of them all but accused somebody in the group of murdering Saunders," Leif went on.

He paused when Megan shot him a look. "You don't think that happened, do you?" she said.

"Considering the blizzard, I'm guessing it was the ice on the streets."

She nodded. "Even if he's just looking for the hacker

in the group, Matt's going to need more than a list of suspects. He's too—"

"Honest?" Leif suggested when she hesitated.

She shrugged. "Close enough. I was actually thinking along the lines of straightforward and naive."

"I was wondering if you wanted to come in for a subtle bit of help," Leif said.

"How?" Megan asked bluntly.

"Maybe we can come at this from the Callivant side. P. J. Farris has these tickets for a Junior League formal. Nikki Callivant's supposed to be there, with several other members of her family—"

"You are obsessing on her!" Megan accused.

"No, I'm not," Leif replied, " 'cause I'm not going to be there. My folks have grounded me, remember? But I still think Nikki is our closest connection to the family. She's our age, and while she doesn't hang in any of our circles, I expect she'll talk with P. J."

"A Callivant and a senator's son. Yeah, that might work." P. J. tended to kid about the fact that his dad was in the Senate—"the honorable member from the great state of Texas!" But between his stunning good looks and his political connections, P. J.'d have no trouble catching Nikki Callivant's attention. Megan looked suspiciously at Leif. "And where do I come in?"

"Well, P. J. could use a date—" He hurriedly put up his hand before Megan could explode. "And I don't think it would be a bad idea to double-team Nikki. At worst, you could play good cop/bad cop with her."

"With P. J. playing the good cop," Megan growled.

"Well, I don't have to worry about pushing any buttons with Nikki-baby's temper. I'll just mention your name."

"Glad to be of service," Leif said with an ironic smile. "Both for the button—and for finding you a way to get some use out of that gown you bought for the winter formal."

•   •   •

Matt had just enough time after getting home from school to have a glass of milk. Then Father Flannery was at his door. "I had to rearrange my schedule for this," Flannery said. "I certainly hope we'll be able to catch all these people in one afternoon."

"Let me finish this note to my folks, and then we'll be off," Matt promised.

The priest hadn't been surprised when Matt called him this morning. Matt suspected that Flannery knew what he had done at the meeting of the suspicious sleuths. Why else had he made sure that Milo Krantz had been marked by the virtual champagne?

While he scribbled on a piece of paper, Matt reached into his knapsack and handed over a printout. The list was simple—proxy, real name, and address.

"I put them in order of nearest to farthest," Matt said.

Father Flannery grunted as he read. "There's certainly enough ground to cover."

"First on the list is Harry Knox, aka Milo Krantz," Matt said. "He's close by."

"Then the pair pretending to be the Slimms—on the edge of Georgetown, and the fellow proxied up as Lucullus Marten in Virginia." The priest watched as Matt attached his note to the refrigerator with a magnet. "No time like the present, I suppose."

Although their first stop wasn't all that far away, getting there meant crossing an invisible line—the border of the beltway. Named for the ring of parkways around Washington, these suburban towns had once been prime real estate. But that had been years ago. As conditions had improved in Washington, "urban problems" moved to the outer towns, who soon didn't have the police, social services—or the tax base—to handle them.

The town where Harry Knox lived didn't even have the funds to take care of its streets. Huge patches of ice still hadn't been cleared away. They looked like frozen lakes surrounded by a treacherous terrain of cracks and potholes in the pavement. Father Flannery had to drive carefully to keep from skidding his way to their destination.

Once it had been a "town house development," homes for the young professionals—would-be "beltway bandits." The place had been put up quickly, and now its shoddy construction showed. Tiles on the roofs were cracked or gone. Patches of brick were discolored, as if the walls had caught some skin disease. Some windows even had plywood in them instead of glass. The original homeowners had obviously been replaced by renters. A forlorn air of decay hung over the place. On what had once been lawns, children's footprints had scuffed away the thin coating of ice and snow to reveal bare dirt.

Most of the original address plaques had disappeared, replaced with glued plastic numbers or tacked-up cardboard handwritten signs. The doorway Matt and the priest sought didn't even have that. They had to guess they had the right place, counting up and down from the neighbors' numbers.

The doorbell didn't ring. Matt gently eased the storm door open—it looked ready to fall off in his hand—and knocked.

"Gimme a minute!" a female voice yelled from inside. Shortly afterward, the inner door opened, and Matt was confronted by a woman in a housecoat. She carried a baby in one arm. A two-year-old peeked from behind her left leg.

"Whatever you're selling, I'm not buying any," the woman said. Her eyes fastened on Father Flannery's Roman collar. "And that goes double for holy rollers." She paused for a second, and then a sickening smile spread over her fleshy features. "Unless, of course, you're here about our financial problems. I've applied to several churches for help. It's all I could do, until the lawyers make my husband do the right thing."

"That would be Harry Knox?" Father Flannery said.

"It was," the woman said. "I threw him out of here weeks ago, and he hasn't been back. The divorce should be a done deal. I'll get the real estate, he keeps the truck and pays to keep us going. But until the checks start coming—"

"Do you know where Mr. Knox is?" Matt interrupted.

When she saw that there wouldn't be an immediate handout, Mrs. Knox's flabby features tightened. "What do you need to bother with Harry for? This is where the money's needed."

"There are things we have to check," Father Flannery put in diplomatically.

"His mail's been going to a truck stop out Fairfax way." The woman spoke angrily. "Place called O'Dell's. I suppose he's livin' it up with some waitress or something."

Catching the change in mood, the infant and the two-year-old began to whimper.

"Shut up, the two of you!" Mrs. Knox snapped at the kids before returning her attention to her unexpected guests. "You go see him and do whatever you got to do. What I need is money!"

Before Matt or Father Flannery could say anything, the door slammed shut in their faces.

Both were silent as they got back into the car. The priest started the engine, and they pulled away.

"Fairfax. That's on the other side of D.C.," Matt said.

"Which will probably make it last on our list," Father Flannery said. A moment or two of silence passed, then he spoke up again. "I haven't read many Milo Krantz stories. Wasn't he a confirmed bachelor?"

"A lot of the old-time detectives were woman-haters," Matt agreed. "Like Lucullus Marten."

"But not like Monty Newman," the priest said with a smile.

Matt shrugged. "The way I read it, Monty liked women too much to settle down with just one. And if what we just saw is typical, he made the right choice."

• • •

They left the beltway for a southbound parkway that finally led into Rock Creek Park, the steep, tree-filled valley that cut Georgetown off from the rest of Washington. Then Father Flannery's car was gently bouncing along the narrow, cobblestone streets, that, along with the eighteenth-century houses, gave Georgetown so much of its charm.

Even the growth of telecommuting and virtual tourism hadn't managed to thin the traffic clogging those streets, however. And parking, especially near Georgetown University, remained an aggravating problem. Matt and Father Flannery faced a stiff walk before they finally reached their destination, a dormitory on the university campus. Leif's tracing program had followed both Mick and Maura Slimm to the student housing here. In real life they were Kerry Jones and Suzanne Kellerman, a pair of college sophomores.

Father Flannery's collar went a long way toward getting them past the resident assistant, and soon they were in Kerry Jones's dorm room. There were two guys in the room, the lanky redhead who answered their knock and the blond young man sitting cross-legged on an unmade bed. The old flatfilm poster taped up over his head was a giveaway clue—it heralded the opening of *That Slimm Fella*, the first Mick and Maura movie.

Jones was a blond guy with a cheerful face, penetrating blue eyes, and patchy fuzz around his chin—a failing attempt to grow a beard. He was built like a football halfback, rather than Mick Slimm's elegant but lethally wiry form.

The young man's eyes sharpened with recognition when he saw Matt. "Can you give us a few minutes alone?" he asked his roommate, who shrugged and went out the door.

"So," Jones said, "you tracked me down. Grab a seat— wherever you can. If I'd known I'd be having visitors, I'd have neatened up the place a little."

The room was decorated in Early Poverty: beds, desks,

and dressers obviously provided by the university—
sturdy, utilitarian furniture built to survive successive
classes of college students. The computer-link couches
were reasonably high-end, but then Matt's own research
into college choices told him that most schools provided
reduced-rate equipment which students could buy.

Father Flannery sat on one of the couches—the one
without the scattering of books and papers—while Matt
perched on the roommate's bed.

"So, you're Kerry Jones," Matt said.

"That's me," Jones cheerfully admitted.

"And, according to our information, Suzanne Kellerman is at class right now," Father Flannery said.

"Okay." Kerry Jones spread his hands. "You found us.
Big deal. Neither Suze nor I think the situation has
changed since the big meeting. We don't see any reason
to join in the defensive alliance your fat friend suggested."

Jones turned to Father Flannery. "Is that what you look
like with your fat suit off?" He pointed to the Roman
collar. "Or is that a new disguise you're wearing? Pretty
sleazy trick to squeeze your way into the dorm."

"I *am* a priest," Flannery said stiffly. "My parish is
about a mile from here. And I'm not Marten. I'm Spanner."

Kerry Jones looked a little shocked. "Sorry, Father. I
didn't expect to be playing out the Van Alst case with a
priest. Not to mention a priest whose proxy uses brass
knuckles."

"I never—" Flannery began.

Matt decided to step in before Jones managed to side-
track their talk into a discussion of the sim.

"We've got a different mystery to deal with right
now—and I hope there'll be no need for brass knuckles."

Jones's face twisted with impatience. "I know I'm not
the nimrod who went hacking into the Callivant files.
And Suze has even less reason. I'm the one who got us
signed up for the sim—for obvious reasons." He pointed

to the poster over his bed, then to the desk beside the window—the one with the more elaborate computer console and the one neat part of the entire room—the ranked racks of computer datascrips climbing the wall. "I'm an old-time film buff. Each scrip contains a flatfilm movie— most of them mysteries. Suze is a . . . good friend."

Girlfriend, Matt instantly translated.

Jones shrugged. "She must like me, because she puts up with watching stuff from my collection. The Slimm movies are our favorites. Suze thought it would be cool to come in as Maura, doing the whole thirties thing, being witty and wearing gorgeous gowns—" He grinned. "As soon as I assured her that everything wouldn't be in black and white."

"Are you sure she'll still like you when that law firm starts putting pressure on her?" Matt asked.

"Suze is pre-law, and she pretty much knows what they can and can't do," Jones replied. "We don't even know if Saunders got his letter off. Even if he did, we've got the best defense. We're innocent."

"And that's enough for you?" Father Flannery burst out. "You don't want to find out who's behind all this trouble?"

Jones looked about to say something, then swallowed his words. "Look, Father," he finally said. "This is no game. In real life, I leave the investigating to the professionals. The cops think that our pal Saunders died in an accident. If the Callivant lawyers want to find the hacker, let them hire somebody to do the job. Suze and I have nothing to hide. They can't find any evidence of something we never did."

His lips curled dismissively. "And if Ol' Fatso is right with his paranoid fantasy about the forces of darkness gathering against us . . . well, it's like I said before. Suze and I can guard each other's backs."

Matt wanted to wipe that arrogant smile off the college kid's face. "Fine—as long as the next 'accident' doesn't take out the two of you together."

"Like that's really going to happen . . . little boy," Jones sneered.

Matt didn't answer. He merely pulled a sheet of paper from his pocket. "Anyway, I'm going to leave a copy of my real name and Father Tim's and the rest of the group's—just in case. If anything happens to us, you ought to know about it."

That jarred Father Flannery. "Are you sure that's wise?"

"Look, if one or both of them are responsible for the hacking, they've got the list already," Matt pointed out. "If not—well, *I* think we should be pushing the free flow of information among the innocent."

Kerry Jones looked at the folded piece of paper as if it were about to bite him. "I don't know what Suze would say about that—it's a violation of privacy."

Matt shrugged as he and Father Flannery got up to leave the room. "Hey, I'm just leaving it there," he said. "I'm not forcing you to read it." And with that he and Father Tim headed off to contact the next name on the list.

9

"You did *what*?" The hologram image of P. J. Farris's handsome face twisted in distress. His words came out more like a yelp.

Leif aimed his best smile at his computer console. "I got you a date for that formal, buddy. Megan O'Malley."

P. J. grabbed at his head as if he feared it would explode. His fingers left his usually perfectly ordered brown hair standing up in spikes. "How could you—what made you think I wanted a date?" he finally sputtered. "I told you about those tickets because I was hoping to dump them on you, not because I wanted to be saddled with—"

"I don't think Megan is into saddling," Leif cut in. "And there was never any hope that I could use the tickets. I'm grounded because of my little collision with Nikki Callivant. But when I heard that she was going to be at this Junior League thing—"

Now it was P. J.'s turn to butt in. "You sicced Megan on me."

"Hey, I felt sorry for her, knowing she had that nice gown going to waste."

P. J.'s expression moved from shock to horror. "Oh, Lord, that's right! She got dumped by that idiot in her homeroom." He shuddered. "And ever since he did that, he hasn't had a day's luck with his computer. Somehow, it manages to catch every virus, every known programming bug comes crawling in, and every piece of useful schoolwork he's done on it has crashed before he could turn it in." The young Texan's blue eyes clung to Leif's face. "Do you realize what you've done to me?"

"I've given you a chance to meet Nikki Callivant," Leif replied calmly. "Her family will probably be at this hoedown as well."

"You expect me to pick up Nikki Callivant with a date hanging on my arm?" P. J.'s gaze sharpened. "Besides, I always thought you kinda liked Megan."

Leif could feel his face getting warm. "This is not a date, Farris. It's an assignment to help Matt. The two of you will be working as a team."

"Wonderful," P. J. groused. "So that's why you stuck me with Ms. Tact, 2025."

Leif couldn't help his grin. "If I'd really wanted to frack you over, I'd have brought Maj Greene into this little party."

P. J. shuddered at the mental image of their group's most outspoken member rampaging her way through a society ball. "Okay," he admitted. "This is slightly better. *Slightly.* And Matt's pulled my grits from the fire more than once. I owe him. What are you expecting us to do?"

"I want you to check out the family that's probably threatening to make Matt's life miserable. Get close and see what the traffic will bear in terms of questioning." Leif tried to keep his voice light, as if this were the easiest thing in the world. "Since Nikki Callivant is about our age, I think she's our easiest connection. Her father doesn't get out in society much. And somehow, I don't think her grandfather would put up with questions about whatever happened to Priscilla Hadding."

"Would Nikki Callivant even know about the Hadding case?" P. J. asked, his expression dubious.

"From what I've read about the Callivants, she seems to be the most decent person in the family—snotty or not," Leif replied. "The press likes her, gives her pretty sympathetic coverage. Lots of charity stuff, you know. Maybe, if she doesn't know about the Hadding case already, you and Megan can get her interested in it."

Leif spread his hands, putting on his most sincere expression. "I'd do it myself, but I've got three strikes against me—I'm grounded, my parents would kill me if I turned up around Nikki Callivant again—"

"And she might kill you the moment she spotted you." Shaking his head, P. J. gave Leif a wry smile. "So what do you think? I'm supposed to charm this girl while Megan hammers her with questions?"

"That sounds as though it might work," Leif said.

P. J.'s smile turned a bit more sour. "You know, once—just once—I'd like to be the bad cop in one of your good cop/bad cop productions."

"It's just that you're such a gentleman," Leif replied lightly. "You always get the plum role. Speaking of which, you'd better call Megan. With only got two days to get ready, she's got a lot to do—hair stuff, and makeup. The least you could do is take care of the other arrangements. You know—transportation, flowers, high-end restaurant reservation beforehand . . ."

P. J. gave Leif a dark look. "One day, Anderson . . . one day . . ."

The traffic thickened again as Father Flannery steered the car toward the Francis Scott Key Bridge. Across the Potomac was Virginia. Inside the car the silence was thick enough to cut with a knife.

Matt couldn't stand it any longer. "Father, I don't think you've said a word since I gave Jones that list," he said. "Is it really such a problem for you?"

The priest seemed to need a moment to unclench his

fingers from the steering wheel. It was safe enough. They'd come to a dead stop somewhere near the middle of the span.

"I've been trying to figure out an answer to that question since we got back in this car," Flannery finally said. "Maybe things are just moving too fast for me. First I'm enjoying an entertaining sim in my all-too-rare free time, then I'm threatened with lawyers, and then a pair of teenagers pierce my privacy as though there's nothing to it. Then your friend gets his hands on a tracking program with an ease that I find somewhat disturbing. And, heaven help me, I end up helping you unmask the other participants in the sim! Now we're trying to talk to them, but you're the only one who seems to be getting anywhere. I'm the grown-up here, but I seem to be following you—a teenage boy—around like a wet-behind-the-ears novice."

"Are you annoyed? Was I stepping on your toes?"

The priest shook his head in bemusement. "No. I'm just shaken up, and unprepared for this, and I think I'm a little envious at the easy way you're handling things."

"Believe me, Father, I'm just feeling my way. Leif and I—and several of our friends—have had a chance to see how the pros do it. We belong to the Net Force Explorers—"

Flannery's head swung toward him. "Net Force is involved in this?"

The blare of a car horn brought his attention back to the road. They rolled ahead for a car length, then stopped again.

"My friends and I are Net Force *Explorers*," Matt quickly explained. "We watch and learn from various professionals in Net Force. Sometimes we do public-service stuff. We don't have any police powers. But we've seen how cases were handled by Net Force Agents."

And sometimes stuck our noses in—when it seemed necessary, he silently added. But this was strictly personal. Right now Matt was just trying to spare himself, his parents, and the innocent sim participants from the consequences of a hacker's actions. And when Leif or anybody else offered help, Matt would accept it gladly.

"My own experience with investigation comes from a lifetime of reading—and what little I managed to do in the sim," Father Flannery admitted ruefully.

"You felt I was giving away clues when I gave Jones that piece of paper?"

The priest hunched a little over the wheel. "Perhaps more like giving away an advantage," he admitted. "You'd found out those names, and Jones hadn't. Knowledge is power. When you pointed that the hacker would have the names already, I felt a little foolish. And when you talked about the free flow of information, I became ashamed of myself. Obviously, I'm not a good detective, Matt."

"I don't know that I am," Matt said, a little embarrassed. "But I do think that all of us—all the innocent parties, at least—will have to work together to identify the bad sport among us, and hopefully get him or her stopped."

"And what happened to Ed Saunders—what you said to Jones—?" Father Flannery flashed Matt a worried look.

"Look, my dad and I found Saunders." Matt began rubbing his arms against a sudden chill. "It had to be an accident—a coincidence. What I said to Kerry Jones was more like a swift kick to his—um, smugness," he finished lamely.

"Tactics"—Flannery smiled—"mixed with a bit of irritation. In my trade, that's all too familiar."

Matt laughed. "Let's hope we do better with Oswald Derbent."

"Also known as Lucullus Marten." They were across the bridge now. Father Flannery gave the car a little gas and began steering a course away from the city.

• • •

In the quiet suburban neighborhood, the house stood out—both as the oldest structure in the area and, probably, as the local eyesore. Most towns would end up debating whether or not places like this should be declared historic landmarks. But Virginia had way too much history already. Unless a famous ancient general had been born in that gaunt-looking farmhouse—or died in there—nobody would be talking about preservation. They'd be more likely to discuss whether it should be bulldozed before it fell down on its own.

The wooden house desperately needed a fresh coat of paint, and several of the window shutters hung at odd angles. Floorboards creaked alarmingly as Matt and Father Flannery stepped onto the porch. But the structure took the weight, and the noise probably saved them the effort of reaching for the doorbell. Matt saw curtains twitch behind one of the windows.

Before Father Flannery managed to pull his finger from the cracked plastic bell button, the front door swung open just a bit. Even the partial view that Matt got showed a man who'd been seriously shortchanged by life. The top of his head barely came up to the level of Matt's shoulder, and the man's flesh seemed to pull extra-tightly over his small, skinny bones. The man had gotten an extra helping of forehead, and his baldness gave the strange impression that his skull had simply outstretched his thinning hair.

Eyes like shiny brown buttons took them in. When they focused on Matt, the pinched features on the man's face seemed to tighten even more.

"You," he said.

"Oswald Derbent?" Father Flannery asked.

"I am he," the man at the door answered. From the first time, Matt caught a connection to the Lucullus Marten he'd known from the sim. Derbent had a surprisingly deep voice for such a slight frame. And his diction was perfect.

"You might as well come in," Derbent growled after

they'd introduced themselves. "I'd almost congratulate you, except that I imagine your success was due more to technology than deduction."

His glare shifted to examine Matt. "No doubt this is due to your ridiculous performance with that champagne bottle."

"Exactly." Matt nodded, surprised to find himself falling into Monty Newman's responses.

"Ah, well. If you've found me, I expect you've found the others. Perhaps now they'll see the advantages of joint action instead of sordid self-interest."

Derbent led them into what once had been the front parlor of the farmhouse. The furniture was old, the upholstery shabby, so the late-model computer-link couch stood out in almost shocking contrast. But Matt barely noticed that at first. What struck him were the walnut bookshelves that covered every wall.

They ran from floor to ceiling, pushing the few other furnishings into a cramped grouping in the center of the room. Even the spaces over and under the windows had been pressed into service, so they seemed recessed in a foot-thick frame of dark wood. The light that came into the parlor had a strange quality, as if they were sitting in a shadow box.

The funereal scene took a moment to get used to. Matt noticed that a pair of floor lamps flanked what looked like the most comfortable armchair, but the dim glow they shed was barely enough to navigate by once the door was shut. The lights should have been using hundred-watt bulbs. Matt figured the output was more on the range of forty.

"Not exactly bright in here," Father Flannery commented, groping his way forward.

"It's sufficient for my needs," Derbent testily replied. "No need to enrich the local utilities." He gestured, a shadowy figure except for those fierce, shining eyes. "I enjoy an economical style of life. My parents passed away, leaving me this house free and clear. Since then,

I've been able to use their legacy and my savings to live as I choose."

Just like the housebound recluse he played in the sim, Matt thought. *What does he raise on the upstairs floor instead of cactus? Dust bunnies?*

Derbent stepped over to the bookshelves most illuminated by the lamps. "Of course, most of my time is taken up with my . . . collection."

That last word got a brief pause and an even deeper pronunciation than usual—the sort of tone people usually reserve for love or religion.

Matt squinted, trying to make out the faded print on the books' spines. What a surprise—old mysteries.

He spotted a familiar title on a paperback, *Triple Jeopardy*. Beside it was a hardcover book, *Too Many Killers*. These were all Lucullus Marten stories. Matt eagerly read on. "Wow! You even have *Death of a Druid*! I never managed to find a library that had that one."

"It's been out of print since the 1970s," Derbent replied. A trace of pride crept into his voice. "Tracking that title down took some effort, but I wanted all forty-seven of the Marten books. Of course, these are just for pleasure, my reading copies. I have a full set in hardcover—mint—safely stored away. Some of those have never even been opened."

So what are they safe from? Matt wondered in puzzlement. *Eye tracks?*

Derbent sat in his chair, a volume in his lap. His hand gently ran over the book's leather cover in the way others might have caressed a loved one.

"Looking back, I suppose it was a mistake to take part in Mr. Saunders's little mystery. But I was eager to put to use what I had learned from years of reading. I had tried my hand at writing some tales of deduction"—his lips pursed in disgust—"but publishers are no longer interested in that sort of story. Bah!"

The hand resting on the book clenched into a fist, then relaxed. "The chance to step into the skin of my hero was most seductive. I enjoyed the experience."

Derbent glanced at Matt. "Despite your youth, you showed a definite flair for extracting information. Quite . . . passable."

Matt couldn't hide his smile at hearing Lucullus Marten's watchword when he praised Monty Newman's efforts.

Derbent's hand tightened again. "And then this nonsense."

"Yes," Father Flannery said. "It only seems to get worse." He hesitated. "Your suggestions about Mr. Saunders's death—"

Derbent smiled. "Were they a ploy to get you and the others to agree to my proposal, or were they motivated by a justified suspicion?" He shrugged. "It may just be the fear of a man who rarely leaves his house. On the other hand, even a paranoid could have enemies. How have the others reacted to being unmasked?"

"We haven't caught up with Milo Krantz," Matt said. "Apparently, he's a long-distance trucker."

"A trucker." Derbent shook his head mournfully.

"The Slimms turned out to be a pair of college students," Father Flannery reported.

"A fair match to the giddiness of the characters." Derbent nodded to the priest. "As Spike Spanner, Father, you personify the golden age principle of the least likely suspect."

"The students—at least the young man, he did the talking—refuse to take part in any effort to find the hacker." Matt took out the list of the sleuths and their alter egos. "I'll leave this with you, no matter what you decide. I already left it with the students."

Oswald Derbent reached for the paper. "I'll join you in your search, although I don't know how useful my support will be."

"It will mean half of us are interested in the truth," Father Flannery said.

"A fine sentiment," Derbent said, "as long as you don't

examine the motives behind it. Mine are simple. The six of us will either be the investigators or the investigated." The little man shook his head. "We face a mystery, but no data—a word I prefer to the traditional *clues*. That means we—and perhaps our truck-driving associate, if he throws in with us—will have to keep digging in one another's pasts until we turn up the telltale fact—or flaw."

Oswald Derbent's dark, shiny eyes had a bitter expression. "One thing I'm sure of—this mystery will be much less enjoyable than the one we signed up for."

"That Derbent really has a way of putting things," Father Flannery said as they drove deeper into the Virginia countryside.

Matt nodded. "For him to play a reclusive genius—maybe it was typecasting."

"What he said about the three of us having to dig—I don't know that I can do it," the priest said.

"Are you going over to Kerry Jones and Suze Kellerman's side—the one that favors ignoring trouble until it goes away?" Matt asked.

"About having someone else do the investigating? It's tempting," Flannery admitted. "But I don't know if anything will be done—or how. Derbent made it clear that he's not leaving his house to pound the pavement for clues. I'm frankly doubtful as to what I can do."

"I think I hear an *and* coming," Matt said.

"That leaves you—and whatever your friends can do—to clear up this mess."

Matt shifted in his seat. "Do you think I'm up to the job?"

"I don't think you should be expected to do it alone," the priest replied. "Perhaps if this Knox fellow goes in with us—giving us a majority of the people involved—we could approach the lawyers, agree to cooperate in an investigation . . ."

Sounds like he thinks Kerry and Suze are the real

hackers, Matt thought. *If the real hacker is one of the others, will they agree?* He glanced over at the man driving the car. *How do I know I'm not riding with the hacker right now? I just don't buy it, though, and I have to trust my instincts. They're all I've got on this case.*

He sighed. "Well, first I guess we'd better see what Knox has to say."

They didn't have many problems finding O'Dell's. There were signs giving the turnoff for miles ahead on the road. Big rigs were parked all around the complex of small buildings. This wasn't just some sort of greasy spoon. The place had pretty much everything a trucker could need—food, a motel setup, gas pumps, even a combination pharmacy and convenience store. O'Dell's was obviously more than the joint in the old joke—the place with the sign that said EAT HERE AND GET GAS.

Matt and Father Flannery stopped by the sleeping accommodations first. They were told the boss was in the restaurant, and nobody at O'Dell's gave out any information without the boss's say-so.

Reaching for the door to the diner, Matt had to jump back as a big, swag-bellied guy came pushing out. The flying door just missed Matt, and the big guy's shoulder brushed Father Flannery aside. Maybe the cloud of beer fumes explained why the guy had to turn making an exit into a pickup game of tackle football.

Matt shook his head as he caught the door on the rebound. He and the priest stepped into the glorified diner and were assaulted by a collection of delicious smells— coffee, pie, bacon, steak . . .

All of a sudden Matt was reminded that it had been a long time since his after-school glass of milk. They asked the counterman if the boss was around, and he replied that she was in the back. "Be with you in a minute."

Father Flannery immediately grabbed a stool and asked for a cup of coffee. After a moment's thought Matt ordered a chocolate shake. A round-faced, heavyset woman brought their orders over. "I'm Della O'Dell," she said. "What can I do for you fellas?"

"Della O'Dell," Matt echoed.

The woman grinned, transforming her face into a thing of beauty. "Great, isn't it? Sometimes I really have to wonder what my parents were thinking."

"I understand you let truckers use your place as a convenience address," Father Flannery said.

"Some, Padre," Della said guardedly.

"It's important that we get in touch with a fellow named Harry Knox—"

"Hard Knocks Harry? He was here just a minute ago." Della turned to the counterman. "Wilbur, where did he go?"

The man held up a bill. "I dunno, but he left a twenty."

"Maybe he went to get something from his rig," Della said. "Hard to miss. It's got a huge red stripe running around the top—"

"Like that truck pulling out there?" Matt pointed to the window. A big rig roared onto the highway, the rumble of its engine making the whole diner shake.

"What in perdition is his trouble?" Della O'Dell wanted to know. "Harry said he was turning down that Florida run. What's he doing now?"

"About fifty-five, I'd say," Wilbur said, watching the truck rapidly disappear.

Matt looked at Father Flannery. "What do you say, Spike?" he murmured. "You up for a high-speed chase?"

The priest shook his head. Instead, he turned to Della. "Is that pie over there as good as it smells?"

A while afterward they were heading back to Washington. "I wouldn't say that was a *complete* loss," Flannery said, patting his stomach.

The hot apple pie—à la mode—had gone down very easily, Matt had to admit. Less satisfying was the reason for the fast exit Harry Knox had pulled. "He must have caught sight of me coming across the parking lot," Matt said.

"In that case, it doesn't speak very well for 'Hard Knocks Harry,' " the priest said. "As the basic manual of my profession says, 'The guilty flee where no man pursueth.' "

"I guess it's just as well we didn't try to pursue," Matt said, gesturing to the slow-moving traffic all around them. "A high-speed chase would have been out of the question in this mess."

They crawled along the road until they reached the Francis Scott Key Bridge, where police officers haloed by the glowing lights of emergency vehicles diverted the traffic to one lane.

"Must have been an accident," Matt said, peering into the glare. "I think a whole section of the retaining wall is gone—"

Then, cocked at a drunken angle, he saw the rear end of a truck trailer sticking up from the water beyond. The cab and engine were completely submerged. But Matt couldn't miss the big red stripe running around under the roof of the rig. Wherever Harry Knox was headed, he obviously wasn't in a hurry now.

IO

Matt couldn't eat supper when he got home that evening—and it had nothing to do with ruining his appetite with pie. He tossed and turned all through the night, and the next morning, even though it was Saturday, he tried Captain Winters's office number at Net Force.

Actually, Matt wasn't surprised when the captain answered. Winters often put in extra hours to clear the week's paperwork off his desk. It was a little weird to see him in a sweater instead of business wear, but the maintenance staff tended to skimp on the Pentagon's heat during the winter weekends.

"What's up, Matt?" The captain's gaze sharpened as he took in the expression on his caller's face. "Or should I say 'what's the matter?' "

Matt tried to tell his whole story—not very coherently, he feared. Words poured from his lips. Winters had to calm him down and asked several questions before he'd finished.

"So, at least two people involved with this sim have died?"

Matt could only nod.

The captain turned away, barking orders to his computer. He continued to stare past Matt's right ear, actually reading a data display that didn't show from the captain's desk pickup.

"I've got the D.C. police report on what happened to Edward Saunders," Winters said. "According to this, the medical examiner found nothing that wasn't consistent with accidental death."

So, Matt thought, *David's dad is going to close the book on that case.*

Another couple of commands, and Winters read silently for another moment. "And it looks as if the police are leaning toward accident to explain what happened on the bridge as well. Driving conditions were bad—ice doesn't melt as easily on bridges as it does on roads."

He looked a little disgusted as he read on. "And among the debris they found in the cab of that truck were several empty beer cans. Mr. Knox apparently had elevated levels of alcohol in his bloodstream. He shouldn't have been behind the wheel."

A sudden image of the beery trucker slamming past him flashed into Matt's mental view. *No shape to drive,* an accusing voice whispered in the back of his head. *And he was running away from you!*

Matt didn't know how he looked, but obviously something of his thoughts showed on his face.

"Are you okay?" Winters asked.

"We had gone down to that truck stop, Father Flannery and I, to try and talk to Knox. He knew what I looked like—I'd showed up for Saunders's virtual meeting without a proxy. What if Knox was sitting there, drinking beer, and saw me coming? Trying to ditch me got him killed!"

Captain Winters shook his head. "There's one thing I learned in combat—never blame yourself for what other people do." Again, he read the invisible report. "In this case, you shouldn't blame yourself at all. One of the other truckers at that diner heard Knox on his wallet-phone. Some sort of rush job had come up. That's why he hurried off."

Matt took a long, shaky breath. "That's a relief," he said. Then he frowned. "I don't suppose we know where he was rushing off to?"

"The police haven't found that out yet," Winters admitted. "But—"

"Doesn't it seem a little funny to you that Saunders and Knox died within just a few days of each other?"

"Between the Marines and this job, some days all I seem to see are coincidences and conspiracy theories. I've seen guys go through complete combat hitches without a scratch—until their last day. I've seen unlucky helicopters whose gunners always got killed. I've had a string of apparent suicides turn out to be murders." He shook his head. "And I've had thirty-seven people named Smith die within three days—and they had all synched in to the same Net site. Our computers popped that one up. We hit it from every direction we could think of."

"And?" Matt asked.

"No family connection, no geographic connection, they didn't even know one another. No record of anything like that happening before, and it hasn't happened since. So far as we were able to conclude, it was just dumb luck. A whole bunch of Smiths had their number come up in the big computer in the sky." Winters leaned toward his pickup, his eyes going for contact with Matt's. "You see what I'm saying?"

Matt nodded. "A pair of people makes for a pretty small sample." He sighed. "I just wish—"

"There's nothing we can do, Matt," Winters said gently. "No evidence of Net crime . . ." His voice trailed off, and he gave another command. "I think I'll just take a look into the hacking complaint regarding those court records, though."

Matt stifled a laugh at that one. Getting Net Force involved in such a small-potatoes case would be like using a shotgun to silence a buzzing fly—overkill to the nth degree.

Now Winters was frowning, staring at his invisible data screen again. "Could you repeat the name of the girl who died?"

"Priscilla Hadding," Matt said. "It happened in Haddington—it's a suburb of Wilmington."

"I'm checking the town, the county, Wilmington city government, and now the state—that's odd . . . there seems to be no mention of intrusion into any court records involving the case—nor of any investigation."

"Shouldn't some cops somewhere in Delaware be doing something?" Matt asked.

The captain shrugged. "When it comes to families like the Callivants, local law enforcement tends to walk softly." His eyebrows rose. "The same probably goes for federal agencies."

"Then I guess the best I can do is hope that nothing else happens to the people from Saunders's sim," Matt said gloomily. Then he sat up straighter. "I'd like to send a copy of my files on the sim and the names and addresses of the people involved to you, though."

He gave a command, and Winters glanced past him again, taking in the new reading matter.

"Who helped you get these—Leif Anderson?" the captain waved a hand. ". . . On second thought, I don't want to know. I suppose I don't want to know what you used to get the names, either."

"Um—probably not," Matt said, silently thanking heaven for such things as small potatoes. "But I know I feel better that you have it."

That evening Megan did her best to make an entrance as she came into the living room. Tonight, P. J. Farris would be taking her to a formal dance. He'd sat talking with her parents while she made her last-minute preparations and rose as she walked in.

"You look—wow—great!" he said, smiling.

She returned the compliment. "So do you."

Both of them avoided the word *pretty*—a sore point with P. J. His good looks had stuck him with too many nicknames like "Pretty Boy"—Megan had called him that more than once herself, when she got mad at him.

Tonight, though, he looked like a teen idol who had escaped from some holodrama or other. His tuxedo fit perfectly and was obviously *not* a rental job.

Megan had gone to considerable trouble, too. Her brown hair, usually on the wild side, had been cut and curled into something resembling stylishness. She really liked her gown, even though it was more classic style than cutting edge. This year's cutting edge had sliced a lot off the top of feminine formal wear, to the point where one of her friends had actually fallen out of her dress at an embarrassing moment during the most recent dance. Megan's gown, which had a close-fitting strapless midnight blue silk bodice that swirled into a deliciously romantic long velvet skirt, showed off just enough of her figure to keep men interested without risking arrest for indecent exposure. Best of all, a little bolero-style jacket made sure she wouldn't freeze her assets off.

P. J. was a good sport, ignoring comments from Megan's brothers and even posing as her dad took way too many pictures. Anything to replace that portrait of her trying to hide her fury while standing beside Andy Moore in his tacky tux. She still wasn't sure he hadn't rented the awful thing on purpose, just to embarrass her.

Instead of a coat, Megan had a fine wool cape her mom had produced from somewhere. She arranged it around her shoulders, holding it together with a silver pin. Then, giving one arm to P. J. and waving with the other, she stepped out the door, heading for P. J.'s waiting limo.

Catching their reflection in the car's window, she had to grin. "We really do clean up well, don't we?"

P. J. gallantly handed her into the car. "Remind me to get a copy of one of those shots from your father," he said. "I want Leif to eat his heart out."

"As if," Megan grumbled, settling onto the backseat. Eager to change the subject, she reached out as P. J. sat beside her. "I think your tie is a little off to the—oh!"

Her attempt to adjust the black bow untied it instead, leaving P. J. with two lank strips of silk dangling across the lace front of his shirt.

He glanced at the door that had just shut behind them. "Well, at least you waited until we got out of your parents' sight before you started undressing me," he said.

Megan shot a horrified hand to her mouth. Then giggles began infiltrating their way from behind its cover. "I-I thought it was one of those one-piece things," she gasped.

P. J. shook his head. "A gentleman is supposed to know how to fix his own tie."

"Do you?" Megan asked. "I mean, did someone else—?"

"My mommy stopped helping me get into my clothes some years ago," P. J. interrupted, straightening out the ends of the tie. Then, trying to use his window as a mirror, he began trying to reconstruct the knot.

When his third attempt failed, Megan timidly said, "You're going to get that all crumpled. May I—?"

P. J. shook his head, leaned back in his seat, closed his eyes, and began working all over again, by feel.

Megan stared in disbelief. "You got it! All you have to do—"

"No!" P. J. said, bringing up both palms to block Megan's helping hands. Then, a bit more gallantly, "If you don't mind, I'll adjust it myself."

Arriving at an old-line hotel in downtown Washington, they walked under the canopy on an actual red carpet and took the elevator to the ballroom floor. They checked their coats, P. J. gave in their tickets, and Megan stood in the doorway, staring at the crowd. It was amazing—horrifyingly dowdy dresses decked out with drop-dead jewelry, doubtless family heirlooms dragged out once in a great while from safe-deposit vaults. Some of the men had tuxes that made that rag Andy Moore had worn look like high fashion.

And then there were the young women in the kind of outfits that Megan had only seen in magazines and HoloNews fashion coverage. Her fingers picked at the hem of her jacket. All of a sudden, her gown didn't seem as great as it had back home.

What am I doing here? a panicky voice demanded in the back of her brain. *This is just like the Leets looking down their noses at me in school—only multiplied by about fifty years and a thousand percent snobbishness!*

P. J. appeared beside her, taking Megan's arm. "I heard that gasp. Pretty awful, isn't it?" he commented in a low voice. "It could be worse. At least most of the money here is old and a bit reserved. Back home we have the good ol' boys in the gold lamé western-cut dinner jackets, and lots of women with big hair and rhinestones. Or was that even what you were gasping at? Maybe you were just reacting to what the band is doing to that song?"

Megan finally focused on the twelve-piece combo at the front of the room. They were playing away, the sound getting muddled with the noise of a thousand conversations. Even listening carefully, it took her a moment to decipher the music. It had been a hot tune a couple of months ago. Everybody had been downloading it. As for this version, however . . . well, she'd heard better in cheap elevators.

Shaking his head, P. J. began walking in. "And this is probably the best thing we're going to hear tonight," he warned.

Megan found herself laughing. What did she have to fear from people with such awful taste in music? Bring the snobs on!

Even so, she had to hand it to P. J. As he began introducing her to people in the crowd, he slowly worked his way up the social ladder. In between dances and breaks for what the Junior League thought of as refreshments, he brought Megan to congressional aides and some lobbyists. Next she met social and political friends of P. J.'s father. Then came members of Congress, and finally some of Senator Farris's colleagues.

At last they joined one of the crowds swirling around the celebrity guests. Even the rich and socially prominent liked to suck up to famous people, Megan discovered—at least, the younger generation did. P. J. steered her expertly to the eye of the storm.

For all intents and purposes, it was a reception line. Nikki Callivant, doing her best to be gracious in a gown that only brilliant engineering design could have kept in place, was shaking hands and chatting with a pair of women in equally modish costumes. Beside her, a tallish, pleasant-faced man with gray hair pressed the flesh with the women's husbands. Behind them was a burly, balding red-faced man who looked as if he couldn't wait for this hoedown to be over.

P. J. aimed first for the tall man. "Senator," he said, shaking hands.

"As in once and future," the man replied with a laugh.

"I remember my father introducing me to you on the Senate floor," P. J. went on. "I'm P. J. Farris."

"Trav Farris's son?" The man's interest now matched his geniality. "Well, you've certainly grown." He rolled his eyes. "To state the obvious. And who is this delightful young lady?"

"Megan O'Malley."

"Walter G. Callivant. A pleasure to meet you." The older man took Megan's hand in a warm clasp. It took her a moment to match the smiling face before her with the rather harassed figure in HoloNews clips that had provided so much material for the comedians.

Well, he didn't spill a drink on me, or spit when he talked, Megan thought.

"Some people get depressed when they discover that colleagues' children have grown up behind their backs,"

Callivant said. "I like to think of it as a glimpse into the future." He shook his head. "I also hope that wasn't something from an old campaign speech. Let me introduce you to someone more your own age. Nicola!"

Walter G. stepped over and neatly disentangled Nikki Callivant from the pair of fawning socialites. "May I present my granddaughter, Nicola. Nikki, meet Megan O'Malley and P. J. Farris. I worked with this young man's father, Trav Farris."

"The senator from Texas," Nikki said quickly. "Nice to meet you."

"Right—I'm sure it's very nice." P. J. laughed, looking at the zoo around them.

Nikki's smile broke through her company manners. "At least my grandfather knew you." Megan could barely hear her voice over the chatter around them.

"How can you stand it?" Megan asked.

Now Nikki's smile became rueful. "This event will help several charities my family supports, and the money is desperately needed. If I have to risk pneumonia and smile until my face hurts, it's a small price to pay. It's the least we can do—"

And it's an election year, Megan thought. She almost yelped as an elbow caught her in the ribs. There were other people who wanted to touch a Callivant, and Megan and P. J. were holding up the line.

"Perhaps I'll see you later," Nikki called after them. Then she turned to the next set of hand-grabbers.

"If I hold my breath till that happens, my face will match my gown," Megan muttered as they made their escape. "Nikki and her grandfather are doing better business than some of the refreshment stands."

"Which would you rather have?" P. J. asked mockingly. "The glow of personal contact with the Callivant clan, or mediocre domestic champagne and a scrap of mystery meat in puff pastry?"

"They're on display like prize hogs."

"It's for charity," P. J. said. "And I suppose it beats

sticking your head through a hole in a sheet and having people throw pies at you."

"I suppose it's also for politics." Megan glanced at him. "Walter G. wants his party's nomination for senator."

They both looked at the older man shaking hands with lots of young and not-so-young Junior League supporters. "I'd say he's doing pretty well with the trust-fund constituency," P. J. observed.

"But they're cramping our style," Megan complained. "How are we even supposed to talk to her again?"

"As opportunity allows." P. J. sighed. "Look at me— here I am, wasting all those good-cop lines I've been studying. Shall I practice them on you? Would you like to dance?"

Megan's opportunity to talk to Nikki came, of all places, in the ladies' room. The winter prom had shown her some of the dangers of high formal fashion. Besides nearly falling out of some of the more extreme gowns, girls had tripped on their long, swirling skirts or sprained their ankles falling off the high, slender spike heels that were all the rage.

Destroyed hems, ripped hose, and torn seams were common. Sometimes they'd speared the fabric with their own high heels, other times a clumsy date had stepped on their skirts, sometimes a stranger got too close at the wrong moment. But the worst combination had proven to be haute couture and plumbing. One girl had even flushed a bit of her skirt down the toilet, which had left her stuck in the ladies' room and had caused a flood. Almost everyone had to depend on friends for help in either temporarily escaping from or rearranging their fashionable formal wear in "the ladies' lounge."

High society had the same problem as high school prom girls, Megan discovered, but the hotel provided female attendants to give whatever assistance was needed.

Unfortunately, at that moment the system had broken down—or maybe some designer's creation had. A young woman was screaming that one of the attendants had destroyed her new Modeschau gown while helping her into the stall.

Women in formal gowns and uniformed attendants alike were all gawking at the disturbance, so that everybody except Megan missed Nikki Callivant about to have her own fashion disaster. Megan acted fast—two quick steps and a grab prevented the socialite's gown from being destroyed that evening. Megan helped a pink-faced Nikki get back to normal, and a few minutes later they were in front of the big plate-glass mirror repairing their lipstick and making a few final adjustments to their dresses before heading back out to the ballroom.

Nicola Callivant's face was still a little flushed from her recent misadventure. "Thanks again for your help. I wish I had the sense to wear something like you have on—something sensible—"

"You mean something off-the-rack and unfashionable?" Megan asked as they left the lounge for the ballroom.

The other girl blinked, then cocked her head. "You say what you think, don't you?"

"Even when people don't want to hear it," Megan agreed. "For instance, did you know that P. J. and I are friends of Leif Anderson?"

Nikki Callivant nearly had another disaster, tripping on her skirt in midstep. "What?"

"We all belong to the Net Force Explorers," Megan went on as if nothing had happened. "Leif's not as bad as you seem to think. He has his good points. For instance, he's very loyal to his friends."

"How nice." Nikki Callivant's voice grew cold.

Megan plowed right ahead. "We're trying to help another friend who seems to have gotten into some trouble with your family. A classmate of mine from Bradford Academy—a guy named Matt Hunter. He was playing in a mystery sim that turned out to touch on a forty-year-old skeleton in the Callivant family closet. The death of a girl named Priscilla Hadding—"

Nicola Callivant had stopped asking questions or making comments. She just stared at Megan, her mouth open.

"Is there a problem here?" The interrupting voice was gruff, but the burly man's moves were smooth as he moved to separate Megan and Nikki. It was the balding, iron-haired man who'd stood in boredom behind Nikki and her grandfather. He didn't look bored now. Icy blue eyes backed up his question.

"It's nothing, Grandpa," Nikki said. "Just the usual madhouse in the ladies' room."

The older man took her arm. "I don't know why you object to having a female operative come along—" Megan lost whatever else he said in the party noise as they walked away.

Grandpa? Megan thought. *Who the frack is that guy?*

Even without being grounded, Leif wouldn't have gone far from his computer console tonight. He was impatiently waiting for a report from P. J. and Megan.

The call came much earlier than he expected, though. In spite of that, the call announcement chime had barely sounded once before Leif shouted at his computer to accept the connection.

Megan O'Malley's face swam into focus in the holographic display over the console—as did the rest of her upper half.

Leif sliced the air with a loud wolf whistle. "Whoa! Nice dress, O'Malley!"

She gave him a look and pulled the little jacket she wore more tightly closed. "We decided to bail early on the Junior League thing. It's a school night, after all."

"At least you weren't thrown out," Leif said. "Or nearly drowned. Any luck in bumping into the snobby one?"

"Most of the time we saw her, she was trying to be polite and seemed quite human," Megan replied. "I had a couple of minutes alone with her, rattled her cage a bit, and got a brief taste of what you received."

"What did you do?"

When he saw Megan's suspiciously sweet smile, Leif braced himself. "I took your advice," she said, "and told her that you were a friend of mine. She began to get a little snotty, but that changed after I mentioned Priscilla Hadding."

Leif leaned toward her image. "Don't stop there."

"It shook her up. But I didn't get the chance to take advantage of that. This older guy stepped in and hauled her off. That was the last shot I got at her." Megan shrugged. "Another reason to blow out of there early."

She squinted at him. "We'd already met Nikki's grandfather."

"Walter G.?"

Megan nodded. "But the guy who showed up to rescue her—she called him Grandpa, too. What gives with that?" Before he could make a comment, she hurried on. "Yeah, of course she has two sets of grandparents. But now that I come to think of it, I've never seen nor heard of anybody but the Callivant side—and I looked in all the same books you did."

"You'd have to look farther afield than that," Leif said, "if it's who I think it is. This guy. Balding, iron-gray hair, built like a football player gone to seed?"

Giving him a suspicious glance, Megan nodded. "Sounds like you know him."

"As it happens, I do. That gentleman is her *great*-grandfather, Clyde Finch. He's the head of security for the Callivant clan."

"He looks only a little older than Walter G."

"Less than twenty years older, as a matter of fact. Clyde was divorced and came to live in the Callivant compound with his sixteen-year-old daughter Marcia when he took the job as head of security. Less than a year later Walter G. Callivant married Marcia Finch. It was a big, but well-hushed, scandal. Walter G. was all of nineteen at the time, and Marcia was barely seventeen."

"Nnggggyuck!" Megan said in disgust. "Marriage at that age! She was only as old as we are! What was that all about?"

Leif shrugged. "I can think of at least two reasons, one of them being undying love at first sight. As for the other major possibility—well, the math supports it."

She gave him another look. "I can only imagine." Then she looked thoughtful. "We really don't see much of Grandma Callivant in the popular press, do we?"

"Only photographed in carefully controlled family gatherings," Leif said.

"Sounds like that happens to a lot of Callivant women." Megan sounded grim. "What have they got in that compound, a harem?"

"Find out, in *Secrets of the Rich and Well-Guarded*!" Leif replied in his best holo-announcer's voice. "Speaking of well-guarded, you might enjoy this historical footnote. Can you name the first cop on the scene in Priscilla Hadding's death?"

"Was that in the Herzen book?" Megan asked. "I didn't read that one."

"You didn't miss much," Leif said. "But the fact was mentioned in passing. The cop, by the way, was a fellow called Clyde Finch."

Megan's eyebrows rose. "As someone in Matt's ill-fated sim might say, 'Is this a clue?' "

The Washington weather was no longer icy. It had gone back to the usual winter standard—mild, gray, and damp—when Matt set off for school the next morning. Even though Bradford Academy was far away from Foggy Bottom, wisps of the gray stuff floated past the windows of the autobus Matt rode on the way to class.

Matt's morning turned out to be equally gray. The problems that had haunted him lately had eaten into his study time. He was completely unprepared for the chemistry pop quiz. And he'd barely skimmed the reading for English—which showed all too obviously in class discussion. All in all, his morning's academic performance would have won him an Oscar for the role of Least Prepared Student of the Year.

As soon as he finished eating lunch, Matt headed outside. The weather hadn't improved any, but he found himself in need of some fresh air.

Matt was standing in the parking lot, looking up at the cloudy sky and thinking that he ought to hit the library before the afternoon nailed him, too, when Andy Moore appeared at his elbow.

"Hunter, you sly devil, you," Andy said in admiring tones. "You didn't tell us you'd made a new conquest."

"What are you talking about?" Matt snapped, not in the mood for his friend's clowning.

"Your new girlfriend stopped by in her car." Andy jerked his head in the direction of the street, where a small knot of guys clustered around a gleaming double-parked car. "She specifically asked for Matt Hunter—hey! I heard her!" he protested as Matt swung on him.

"If this is some stupid prank—" Matt began as he headed for the group, Andy trailing behind.

"If it is, it's not one of mine," Andy assured him. "I just wish I'd thought of it," he added in an undertone.

Gritting his teeth, Matt reached the group around the car. Then he saw why so many people were there, gawking. It was a brand-new bronze Dodge concept car, one that looked as if it had just rolled out of the pages of the latest car netzine. Half of the guys were checking out the car. The rest were staring in disbelief at the driver.

She wore a denim jacket, the kind that came lined with an old horse blanket. Matt could tell, because it was way too large on her, and she'd rolled back the sleeves. A bilious green scarf was wound around her neck and up to her chin, and the hat she wore defied all attempts at classification. It was hand-knitted and shapeless, covering all of her hair. The color was somewhere between brown and orange, and the knitter had tried to end up with a flower at the top, but had failed and turned it into a sort of blobby pom-pom.

In spite of the clouds the girl wore sunglasses. Matt's grandmother once had a pair like them—they were built to go on over regular eyeglasses, and they hid the top third of her face as effectively as a mask.

Matt looked hard at what little of the girl's face that remained uncovered, trying to find some feature he could recognize. *Do I know anybody who'd rig themselves out like this for a gag?* he wondered. *Megan? Maj Greene? Who'd put them up to it? Andy swears this isn't one of his gigs. Who else? Leif? Nah, not his style.*

Unable to come up with an answer, and positive this was about to blow up in his face, Matt pushed forward. "I'm Matt Hunter," he said. "Who are you?"

The girl didn't answer, but for a brief second, she raised the sunglasses from her face. Behind the big, clumsy lenses were a pair of beautiful eyes so blue they were almost violet.

Matt remembered Leif describing eyes like that—and on whom. Without another word, he got into the car.

Nikki Callivant started the engine and pulled away down the street. "It seems I need to talk to you," she said in a toneless voice.

"Not for too long, I hope," Matt said, glancing at his watch. "I need to be back in class in about twenty minutes."

"Is there someplace nearby where we can stop?"

"Rock Creek Park isn't too far away," Matt replied. "We could probably find a place to pull up and not even have to leave the car."

She nodded and began steering the car, following Matt's directions.

"I guess I have to congratulate you on your—um—disguise," Matt said as they parked.

"It's something my mother taught me. It distracts people from noticing one's face—especially the press. Your hat can never be too ugly." She gave him a smug smile. "I picked this stuff up at a resale shop."

Matt glanced again at her crowning glory. "I hope they—er—fumigated it before they put it out for sale."

Instantly Nikki tore off the knitted monstrosity. Her light-brown hair flew around her face, and the sunglasses tumbled into her lap.

"Well, there was an honest reaction, at least," Matt said. "What do you need to speak to me about?"

"I met a friend of yours last night," the girl replied. "She said you were in trouble with my family. Something about a mystery—and an old family problem."

"Please understand, I didn't set out to get in trouble with your family," Matt began. "Nor did any of my friends. We were just playing a game. This fellow developed a new mystery sim, but he based it on an old case."

Nikki made a face. "I can guess. The situation in Haddington, all those years ago. I don't know why we didn't just close down the house there. Some adviser or other probably thought it would look bad. A tacit admission of responsibility."

The girl's delicate features froze into an even more bitter expression. "As children, we were coached to stay well away from poor, half-crazy Mrs. Hadding. The police and public prosecutor won't talk to her anymore. If the media even discuss what happened, they call it a 'cold case.' More advisers at work. Public relations. No one can disgrace the Callivant name."

She shook her head. "Even with the assassinations, there are four generations of Callivants in our house. Maybe that's too many. It's made us—well, I don't know what it's made us."

"I know what some people would say," Matt said.

"People!" Nikki scoffed. "They say that public service is my family's business. But if it is, it's only true for the boys. I thought things might have changed when my father didn't run for office. But, of course, he went to work for the government."

"What *does* your dad do?"

"National security," Nikki replied. "Threat analysis, covert this, international that—*we* never get to hear about it."

"He's a what—a spy?" Matt couldn't believe what he was hearing.

"According to my dad, he drives a desk and spends a lot of time worrying about budgets."

So did Captain Winters, Matt suddenly thought. Although sometimes his days got a bit more exciting.

"Whatever your father does, it sounds like another road to power," he finally said.

"Some power." Nikki's lips tightened. "Dad might have escaped some of the family traditions, but he expects me to follow right in line—making the perfect appearances at the right parties with a smile plastered on my face and lots of Callivant charm."

She thumped her chest. "I want to be the Callivant woman who runs for something instead of standing gracefully at somebody else's campaign kickoff. I've got girl cousins who could do just as good a job as the guys in the family. But you'll never hear about them. No public arguments. Family solidarity." She nearly spat the words. "Nobody dares disgrace the Callivant name."

"Or gets away with it?" Matt asked.

She didn't reply to that comment, confusion all too evident in her blue eyes.

Matt went on to describe the strange deaths of Ed Saunders and Harry Knox.

Nikki Callivant shrank away from him in her seat, those strange blue eyes growing wider. "That's crazy," she said. "My family uses lawyers, P.R. people—sometimes strings are pulled. But you're suggesting—"

"I'm just asking if you don't think it's a strange coincidence that two people connected to a small sim based on your family scandal died within a week of each other,"

Matt cut in. He shook his head. "I'm not accusing your family of anything. But I don't know what's going on, and it makes me edgy. Maybe they were accidents. If so, I'm sorry I disturbed you with this. I suppose I should be glad you went out of your way to talk to me, even if I may be saying things you don't want to hear."

"I've been getting a bit of that lately," Nikki ruefully admitted. "Most of it from friends of yours. But it comes along at a time when I've been asking a lot of questions about my family—I guess I'll just have to add these questions in with my own."

She reached under the denim jacket. "I really wish you hadn't used that fumigation line. Now I'm itching like crazy." Still scratching, she pulled out of the parking place and headed back to the school.

At least, Matt thought, she didn't lose control of the car while she drove him back to school one-handed.

Matt was in his room, working on his homework, when the chimes of an incoming call rang out. He closed out his classwork file and ordered the computer to make the connection.

Captain James Winters's face appeared over the console. "Matt, something turned up in relation to those—ah—cases you mentioned to me."

"New information?" Matt eagerly leaned forward.

"More like old information." Winters ran a hand over his chin. "I decided to run a check on the names you gave me, to see if any of those people had a criminal record."

"And Harry Knox did?"

"A juvenile record. It seems back in 1999 Knox was a Script Baby."

Matt blinked. "A what?"

"He was seventeen at the time, exploring the early version of the Net, and found a crude set of hacking tools. They were called 'scripts,' developed by talented, or at least successful, crackers for use by less experienced—even inexperienced—would-be hackers."

"Was Harry Knox experienced?"

"No. That's probably why he got caught. His incompetence is probably what saved him. He wasn't able to do much damage, and the courts were disposed to be lenient with young people on a first offense."

"Anything else?" Matt asked.

"Nothing that we found out," Winters replied. "Maybe he was scared straight. On the other hand, once a hacker—"

"Always a hacker," Matt finished the saying.

"Among the things we recovered from the wreck of his truck was a laptop computer," Winters went on.

That would either put Knox way on the trailing edge of technology, or on a recent dead end. Leif's father had tried to revive the idea of portable, full-powered units, but people were happier with their home consoles and their little palm computers. People who liked playing with techno-toys went for the machines, however. A lot of kids from Net Force had picked up laptops at a deep discount—superbrains like David Gray. "Old or new?" Matt asked.

"It was a late-model unit, damaged in the crash and the dunking," Winters said. "A police technician noticed a certain amount of wear and tear on the input/output connections. Apparently when he was on the road, Knox plugged the laptop into motel systems rather than networking with his home computer."

"That would argue a certain amount of technical ability," Matt offered.

Winters nodded. "Which would seem to point to him as the hacker in your group of sim enthusiasts." He frowned. "But it only suggests his guilt. There's no hard proof."

And since there was no hard proof of hacking—not even a legal complaint—Net Force couldn't get officially involved. Winters had probably pushed the investigative envelope just by looking into the past of the late Harry Knox.

"Thanks for letting me know about this," Matt said.

"For whatever good it does." Winters gave a helpless shrug and signed off.

Seems like I'm collecting a lot of interesting but useless stuff, Matt thought. He filed the latest information in the same mental bin as his conversation with Nikki Callivant. Then he ordered his computer back to the trig problem he'd been trying to solve. Possible clues were always interesting, but right now, homework had to take first priority.

His homework was done and the house was filling with spicy smells when Matt came into the living room that evening. Dad was cooking chicken fajitas for dinner, judging from the scents of frying peppers, onion, and garlic—lots of garlic.

Matt's stomach rumbled, reminding him it had been a while since lunch, as he headed for the main computer console. It was time for the local news.

A holographic projection appeared—the HoloNews logo, clouds floating behind it, while urgent, staccato music came from the living room speakers. "News music," Matt's father had called it once.

"That's a little loud," Matt's mother said, coming in behind him. He told the computer to tone down the sound as she came to stand beside him, wrinkling her nose at the kitchen smells. "Another night at the garlic festival, I see."

Matt grinned and shrugged. "It goes better with his south of the border stuff than with other recipes he tries."

Mom had to agree with that.

A pair of anchorpeople busily went about the business of bringing their viewers up to date on events in the world and in Washington. It must have been a slow news day. Three items, and already they'd turned to the chopper-cam for a fire shot.

Matt's father remembered when the news wars had taken to the air, with the networks and news services hiring helicopters to carry their cameras. Sometimes these flying camera people turned in exciting footage—car chases, train wrecks, huge demonstrations. Most days, however, they wound up showing traffic jams, or on really dull days, the biggest fire in the metropolitan area.

Today was apparently a *very* slow day. The eye in the sky hadn't even been able to find a large factory or apartment building burning away. Instead, they focused on flames roaring through a small wooden home surrounded by suburban houses. From the actions around the pumper trucks below, the local firefighters had given up any hopes of saving the place. Their hoses were aimed at keeping the blaze from spreading to any of the nearby houses.

"The structure dates back more than a hundred and fifty years, always in the same family," the chopper reporter's voice intoned against the faint whine of the engine. "The town of Travers Corners loses a little bit of history today."

Hearing the name of the town jarred Matt into paying more attention. He and Father Flannery had been there, not so long ago.

Matt frowned, trying to reorient himself from the overhead view. Yes. Illuminated in the glare of the inferno, he began to pick out familiar locations. That house over there, and that one . . .

The place being devoured by flame was Oswald Derbent's book-filled home.

Some of what Matt was feeling must have shown on his face. "What's wrong?" his mother asked.

"That." Matt pointed to the HoloNews display. "That house. It belongs to Oswald Derbent—another of the players in the mystery sim. Father Flannery and I were visiting there just the other day."

"I see," Marissa Hunter said, clearly upset by the news. Then, "Where are you going?"

Matt turned back, halfway across the living room. "I think I need to call this in, don't you? To more than one person." He glanced in the direction of the kitchen. "But I'll be done before Dad starts serving supper." The previously savory aromas made his now-leaden stomach simply sink farther.

Stepping into his room, Matt snapped a command at his computer. The call went though, the display over the console swam into focus, and Captain James Winters looked out—still in his office, even at this hour.

The captain's expression went from surprise to concern when he saw Matt.

"That list I sent you—" Matt paused, trying to clear a suddenly hoarse throat.

"Someone else had an—incident?" Winters finished for him. The Net Force agent did not look happy at all.

"Oswald Derbent. HoloNews was just showing pictures of his house—what's left of it—doing an amazing imitation of an open-pit barbecue."

Winters looked annoyed with himself. "I directed my computer to flag any police calls connected to those names," he said. "I'll have to amend that to include all emergency services."

"Can you find out what happened?"

The captain nodded cautiously. "I'll make some inquiries and get back to you. It probably won't be tonight," he warned. "Arson investigations need daylight. And there will be an arson investigation."

"You think there'll be anything by the time I get home from school?" Matt asked.

"Preliminary findings, though not a finished report. I'll call with whatever I can get," Winters promised. "Do me a favor, huh? Be careful! And tell your friends to watch their backs. I'll see what I can do from my end."

They cut their connection, and Matt gave a new series of commands to his computer. Soon he was composing a virtmail message to go out to the other sim participants—proposing a meeting, same place as last time, for tomorrow at six P.M.

He'd just finished when his father's voice came floating back. "Dinner is served!"

I'm betting that my former rivals have Net agents out ready to pounce on any news mentions of our names, he thought, shutting the system down. *But maybe by then I'll be able to tell them a little more than the official story. Free flow of information, after all.*

Bradford Academy's cafeteria was crowded, so Matt decided to do a good deed. He carried David Gray's lunch tray as well as his own. David grimly stumped along on his cane through the mob scene.

"That leg has to be getting better soon," Matt tried to console him.

"The magnetic therapy helps the bones knit faster," David admitted with a grimace. "But it also leaves an itch where I can't scratch."

They reached the table that Andy Moore was holding for them. Matt looked at the two trays, both of which held a sandwich and a soda. "Do you remember which one is yours?"

David sighed. "Does it matter?"

He had a point. They might go to a better-than-average school, but the cafeteria menu was, to put it mildly, lame. Matt gave David his choice and began munching unenthusiastically on a mustard sandwich (at least that was all *he* tasted) when Megan O'Malley plumped down in the seat beside him. A cup of soup slopped on the tray she carried—proof of her intrepid nature, Matt thought. Soup from that kitchen . . . he didn't want to think what was in it.

"How's it going?" Megan asked.

"Not well." Matt took a sip from his gel-pack of soda. "Another name on the List of Ed Saunders has a red mark beside it."

Andy leaned across the table. "Sounds like a good title for one of your dad's books, Megan," he suggested through a mouthful of potato salad.

"The line's been used," David Gray said, taking a taste of his sandwich and making a face. "Just without the name Ed Saunders."

"Forget that," Megan said. "What happened?"

"The guy who played my boss in the sim—his house burned down last night."

Megan shook her head. "I hate to say it, Hunter, but the people from your sim seem awfully . . . accident-prone."

"Not Mister Matt over there," Andy put in. "He's just

rolling in good luck. Did I tell you about the mystery girl in the hot car who came by looking for him?"

"You told *me,*" David said in a long-suffering voice. "Or was it the hot girl in the mystery car you mentioned?"

"Is that for real?" Megan asked Matt.

Feeling the color rise in his face, he shrugged. "Yeah. Not only that, but the girl was a friend of yours—Nikki Callivant."

Megan choked and nearly sprayed Andy with a mouthful of soup. "What? How?"

"I can only give you the *why,*" Matt said. "You mentioned this school and my name when you got together at that charity do. So she came to check me out."

"Sure she wasn't stalking you?" Andy ostentatiously used his napkin to wipe soup droplets off the table.

"Shut up, Moore," Megan and David growled almost in unison.

"I think I'd leave any stalking jobs to her father," Matt said. "He's some kind of muckety-muck in national security."

"That does it!" Andy exclaimed. "For this election, my money will be on Walter G. Callivant."

"You clown," David groused. "Walter G. is a national joke."

"He's really not—" Megan began.

But Andy blithely went right on. "Callivant Lite is the candidate for me. If there are going to be any dirty tricks in this campaign, his side will have access to the best government technology."

He laughed, but quickly shut up when he saw nobody else thought it was funny.

Matt shook his head. *Maybe Andy finally realized what he had to say wasn't exactly in the best of taste.*

"Andy," he said, "for my sake, you'd better hope that you are wrong. Because, otherwise, the list of people in that sim who might be victims is getting awfully short. I could be next."

• • •

Any illusions Andy may have created about luck were quickly dispelled when Matt got home. He opened the door to find a cream-colored envelope lying on the rug—honest to gosh snail-mail! It was so unexpected, he nearly stepped on it.

Then Matt picked the thing up and recognized the return address. He'd seen it on the letterhead of the law firm that had been making Ed Saunders's life miserable.

The other shoe drops, Matt thought gloomily, slitting the envelope open. *It's funny how legal people have stuck to paper. Is it just tradition?*

As he read the couple of paragraphs on expensive stationery, he came up with a new theory. If he'd gotten an electronic letter like this, he'd have simply yelled for his computer to vaporize it.

The letter was addressed both to Matt and his parents, and it demanded that Matt cease and desist all activities which might be construed as harassing the firm's clients (never named), including (but not limited to) attempts at fraternization, telecommunication, and unauthorized abstraction of personal or legal information, to name a few.

And what exactly would authorized *abstraction of information look like?* Matt silently wondered as he read on.

Failure to knock off the above activities, or ones like them, would result in civil action in the courts, and possible criminal complaints, specifically for the continuing offense of felonious use of computer equipment for the purposes of illegally obtaining sealed records pertaining to the firm's clients.

Carefully refolding the heavy document, Matt took it into the kitchen to post on the refrigerator door. Initially he'd intended to raid the fridge as well, but all of a sudden that cafeteria sandwich wasn't sitting too well in his stomach.

The sudden chime of the call announcer sent the paper flying one way and the refrigerator magnet flying another.

"Nerves," Matt muttered as he scooped them both up, plunked the magnet in place, and then went to the living room computer console.

Captain Winters's face appeared when Matt ordered the computer to make the connection.

"Did you have someone watching for me?" Matt asked. "I just got in."

The captain shook his head. "Guess my sense of timing is on today. I managed to get a look at a draft of the report on last night's fire as it came into the Fairfax County Department of Public Safety."

"And?" Matt said.

"It wasn't easy for the investigators to sift through all that debris," Winters went on. "Did you know how much paper was in that wood-frame house? I didn't think people did that anymore. Must have been a regular firetrap."

An image popped up in Matt's mind—all those lovingly shelved books. Oswald Derbent must have skimped his whole life to have collected so many.

Matt forced himself back to the present. "What did the investigators have to say about the cause of the fire?"

"As far as they can determine, the blaze started in one of the lamps in the front parlor—or reading room, or library, whatever you want to call it," Captain Winters said. "The socket on that style of lamp is safety rated for one hundred watts, but there was a two hundred-watt bulb in there. It burned too hot, drew too much power through the wiring, and burst into flames."

Matt put his hands behind his back—he didn't want Winters to know how his fingers were knotting together. "I was in that room just days ago," he said, "and Derbent kept it as dim as a church. He had two lamps, and they were burning *forty-watt* bulbs. I think he considered bright light an extravagance, and maybe a risk that might make his precious books fade. Or maybe he was just cheap—he said he was tight with a buck."

James Winters sighed. "I'll relay that to the authorities, but I doubt they'll act on it. Maybe Derbent got hold of a brighter bulb at a discount store and figured the savings on the price of the bulb offset the higher electricity cost to run it—or maybe he was just going blind from reading all those books and decided to up the wattage."

"Or maybe somebody could have gotten into his house— his nice, dry-as-kindling, wooden, paper-filled house— and stuck an industrial-strength bulb in that old lamp."

Winters's face looked as if it were carved from stone. "Without evidence to the contrary, the public safety people are classifying the fire as accidental."

"I'm sure there'll be plenty of evidence left to support that," Matt said bitterly. "Just like the last two 'accidents.' "

"There were no traces of accelerants, no oily rags, and the only signs that the place had been disturbed could be attributed to Derbent himself, who apparently discovered the fire and called it in."

Matt swallowed. "He was there? The news didn't say anything about Derbent, so I assumed he wasn't home. How is he? How did he take it?"

Winters glanced at an off-screen display. "Oswald Derbent came home from a local store to find the fire pretty well established. He ran inside—why, the local fire people have no idea."

To save his books, Matt thought. "What happened?"

"The ceiling fell on him. Firefighters managed to get him out of the place, and he's in the hospital." Winters hesitated. "He's not expected to make it. If he dies, they plan on ruling it accidental death."

"Uh-*huh*!" Matt said. "Some accident!"

The captain winced as if he'd been punched. "Matt!" He took a deep breath and moderated his tone. "I have to accept what's reported. I can't just throw Net Force into this until we have some evidence of wrongdoing that falls under our jurisdiction."

"And how does it stack up with the incidents I reported to you?" Matt demanded. "Put them together, and I'd say something stinks! Don't you think three people dead out of seven in unrelated accidents inside of a couple of weeks constitutes evidence of wrongdoing?"

"I'm not disagreeing." The muscles along Winters's jawbone bunched. "In this job I'm supposed to think like a cop. But I also have to make sure each I is dotted and every "T" crossed. I can't take official notice of something until I have solid evidence that a crime has taken place. 'Information received' doesn't make the burden of proof."

His eyes speared into Matt's. "I pushed on this one, Matt. Talked to the chief investigator out there. You can imagine how pleased he was to find a federal agent nosing into his case. I told the guy that several of Derbent's associates had recently suffered apparent accidents and advised him to keep a careful eye out for suspicious elements."

Winters shook his head. "And the verdict still came back as 'fire by accidental causes.' "

Matt could see that the man on the other end of the connection wasn't happy. It was obvious that Captain Winters had his hands tied. For that matter, what could Matt himself do?

"I'm glad you tried," Matt finally said. "If I find anything out, I'll get it to you right away. Until then, I hope you're keeping—well, maybe not an eye on us. Call it a Net search." Matt smiled, but there was no humor in his voice as he said, "I'd hate to electrocute myself turning off this system and have you be the last to know."

When six o'clock came, Matt had to force himself to keep the meeting he'd set up. Flying quickly through the garish big-business sector of the Net, he only slowed when he approached the dead storage area. Matt went in carefully, activating the icons for his best dirty-work detectors. The programs found nothing out of place.

Sighing, he slid into the interior of the virtual structure—the dark, echoing warehouse space created by the mystery hacker.

Father Flannery was there ahead of him, standing in the cone of light from one of the overhead lamps. The priest hadn't bothered to don his Spike Spanner proxy. Matt acknowledged the decision with a wry smile. He hadn't come as Monty Newman, either.

"It's a couple of minutes after six," Flannery said, looking at his watch. "How long do you want to allow for people to straggle in?"

Even as he spoke, two more figures suddenly appeared. Matt recognized Kerry Jones. The girl beside him had to be Suzanne Kellerman. Instead of the pert, brown-haired Maura Slimm, Suze Kellerman was tall and blond—and if she'd ever had any of the fictional sleuthette's wise-cracking spirit, it had worn thin in the last few days.

"Both of us have quarterly exams we should be studying for," Jones growled. Apparently, he'd been elected as the couple's spokesperson. "I hope you people won't waste—"

He looked around. "Where's Derbent?"

"He won't be coming." Matt tried to keep his face calm as he made his report. "Not only was his house burned down, but he was injured, too." He had to look away. "From what I hear, he isn't—he won't—"

"Oh, Lord!" Father Flannery was blessing himself when Matt turned back.

Suze Kellerman stared at him with wide blue eyes. Jones's big, genial face looked grim, his mouth a thin white line.

"I don't know what you think you're doing, Hunter, but this time you've gone too far. Calling us here to boast about what you did—"

"What are you saying?" Father Flannery burst out.

"I'm saying that computer-boy over there fits the classic profile for a hacker—someone whose technical ability outstrips his conscience and maturity," Jones accused. "You made a big mistake this time with your order—

excuse me, your invitation. You signed it."

Matt stared at him for a moment, reining in his temper before he spoke. In his experience, answers that began, "Listen, Barfbrain!" usually caused more trouble than they were worth.

"I signed the virtmail so you'd know I *wasn't* the hacker," he finally said. "There's some stuff you ought to hear—information that didn't or won't make the news."

"Information you managed to *find out* . . . somehow." Kerry Jones managed to make the simple statement sound like an accusation.

"Father Flannery knows I'm with the Net Force Explorers," Matt began. "I pulled a few strings on our behalf."

"Net Force is tracking down whoever's behind this?"

Hating to kill the fragile look of hope shining on Suze Kellerman's face, Matt gently said, "I've tried to bring them in, but as far as Net Force is concerned, there's no actual evidence of any Net crime committed." He glanced at Jones. "I did talk to an agent—which you can verify—"

"Count on it," Jones bluntly replied.

"Anyway, he got an advance look at the report from the fire investigators." Matt went on to pass on what Winters had told him.

"Wait a minute!" Father Flannery protested. "We both saw those lamps—if you can call it seeing, considering the dim light they threw. No way on earth could either of them have been burning the bulb you're talking about."

"Just as I said to the Net Force agent." Matt tried to keep the frustration out of his voice. "I'll pass along the answers he gave me, which he got from the fire investigators—a replacement bulb, a mistake—"

"Could he have had the lights dim on purpose that day?" Suze suggested. "Maybe he was hiding his face—"

Matt shook his head. "Not likely. Derbent had no idea

we were coming—" He broke off. "Unless one of you contacted him while we were on the way."

The college kids shook their heads. "Kerry told me about your visit when I came out of class—that's across campus from our dorm."

Jones nodded. "I beat feet over there as soon as you guys left."

"Besides, we saw Derbent's face clearly," Flannery put in. "When he answered the door, he stood in the sunshine. You can't call that hiding."

"Speaking of hiding—or at least, of information a person wouldn't like to get out—one of our detective colleagues had a past." Matt hadn't been sure how he'd handle the information about Harry Knox. Now he made up his mind—full disclosure.

When he finished, Suze Kellerman blinked in bafflement. "Then, Krantz—I mean, Knox—was the hacker. But he's dead. So why are we still getting complaints about hacking?" She pulled out a piece of paper that was all too familiar—a virtual copy of the letter Matt had received that afternoon.

From the way Father Flannery reacted, he'd received the same sort of mail. The priest gave them a sour smile. "If this were a mystery story, the villain would have knocked off Saunders to keep him from exposing his identity along with everyone else's. Knox, because of his own hacker background, would have somehow realized who the hacker was and be trying to blackmail."

"Nice theory." Jones barely kept the sneer out of his voice. "But it doesn't explain what happened to Derbent, does it?"

"Have you got a better explanation?" Matt challenged.

The college guy was definitely wearing his game face as he scowled at Matt and Flannery. "There are two choices here. Either the things that have happened really are all accidents, or somebody's making them happen." Jones took Suze Kellerman's hand. "If they *aren't* accidents, from what I see, that means one of you two is a killer."

For a second Matt glanced at Father Flannery. The priest was outraged. Then Matt swung back to look at Jones. *You know what they say,* he thought. *The best defense is a strong offense.*

Suze unexpectedly broke the standoff. "I don't know what is going on here," she confessed, her voice shaking. "Coincidence, or—whatever."

Then she began to cry. "I—I just want it to stop!"

Matt silently watched as Jones folded his arms around Suze, trying to comfort her. Father Flannery's face was a little pinker—obviously, he empathized with the girl.

If that's acting, she has some major awards in her future, Matt thought.

Kerry Jones had some tissues out and was trying to coax Suze back to calmness. Right now, he didn't look like someone who could pull off a string of cold-blooded "accidents" to hide his guilt.

Jones was right about one thing. The circle of suspects kept shrinking and shrinking. And none of the people left struck Matt as likely cold-blooded, efficient killers. What did that leave them with, then? A nasty set of coincidences heightened by paranoia and scary letters from lawyers?

Matt shook his head as if a tiny buzzing insect were trapped in his ear. No! There *was* a hacker—or, perhaps, there had been one among the sim participants.

Still sniffling, Suze took her boyfriend's hand. Jones glared furiously at Matt as the two of them disappeared.

Father Flannery spread his hands in a gesture of hopelessness and cut his connection, too.

Alone, Matt felt his lips curve in an ironic smile.

The Callivant lawyers shouldn't waste their time badgering us to find out who the hacker is, he thought. *They should just wait to nail the last of us who is still standing!*

13

The lobby wasn't exactly bustling. But there were enough people walking past Matt to the visitors' desk, getting oversized passes, and boarding the elevators for the floors above.

Matt, however, had nowhere to go. The hospital clerk had just turned down his request for a pass. *After all my research,* Matt thought, *that's one bit I never thought to check.*

He'd spent every free moment in school today working the Bradford Academy computer system, trying to get more information about the fire that had burnt out Oswald Derbent's home. Along the way, he'd picked up the fact that Derbent had been brought to the burn unit at George Washington University Hospital.

So, when classes ended, instead of going home, he headed in the opposite direction, south and east to Foggy Bottom. Here was the hospital, there was the visitor's desk—but passes were only for family members.

You should have thought of that, Matt accused himself. *Derbent's situation is worse than critical.*

He wanted to do *something*, not just head back with his tail between his legs. But a get-well balloon or flowers seemed like a pretty empty gesture.

The last thing Matt expected was a hand on his shoulder. He nearly jumped out of his skin as he whipped around to see Father Flannery.

"I thought it was you," the priest said.

"My school isn't all that far away." Matt shrugged, feeling awkward. "When I learned that Mr. Derbent was here—I thought maybe I could visit him. But they wouldn't let me in."

Flannery nodded. "My collar cut no ice with them, either. But they gave me some information."

He sighed. "Derbent is in one of the hyperbaric oxygen modules—that's the best hope, given the severity of his burns. If they can keep his condition stabilized long enough, they'll try for synthetic skin grafts. But they aren't optimistic."

Matt nodded. Derbent wasn't a big man, and he was no kid.

"There's a small chapel." Flannery nodded off to one side. "I was in there praying for him." The priest hesitated, then went on. "Before that, I was visiting with Mrs. Knox."

"Those—both—were kind things to do," Matt said.

"As we said before, they come with the job." Flannery looked embarrassed. "The poor woman is a wreck. She has no idea whether her husband was keeping up his insurance, and there's still no money coming in. There are children to be fed, and a roof to be kept over their heads—" The priest shook his head. "I gave her some advice, suggested some places she could go. She was almost pathetically grateful. She talked a great deal—I suppose she was glad to have a friendly ear."

He grimaced. "But it seems I haven't quite shaken off the influence of Spike Spanner. I asked some questions, too."

Matt sighed. "And did you dig up any clues?"

"I suppose you'd call it something more like back-ground information. It seems Hard-Knocks Harry was a bit of a dreamer," Father Flannery said. "He talked big, but never accomplished anything."

"He wound up with that big rig."

"Financed with a legacy from his uncle," Flannery said. "When he wasn't on the road, he was synched into his computer. After his juvenile brush with the law, Knox apparently fancied himself as quite the outlaw. He liked sims about hacking. He and the missus apparently had some arguments about it. She didn't want him leading the children astray."

"So he decided to be a great detective instead?" Matt asked.

The priest nodded. "But that wasn't the kind of reform Mrs. Knox had in mind. She's a bit of a technophobe. Computers give her the creeps. She complained about her husband lying around, connected to what she called a 'soulless machine.'"

"Maybe she had a point," Matt suggested.

"If she went too far in one direction, Knox went too far in the other. He was determined to solve the fictional Van Alst case. In fact, he hinted that it might lead to real-life benefits."

Matt paused for a second. "The hacking."

"The widow Knox doesn't know about that," Flannery said, "and I didn't tell her. But it sounds like he may have been behind it."

"Well, we'll certainly never find out." Matt shrugged.

Now it was the priest's turn to pause.

"We might," said Father Flannery. "The arguments over Hard-Knocks Harry's virtual life ended with his wife throwing him out of the house." He glanced at Matt. "She also disconnected his computer."

Matt stared. "What?"

"She had some muddled fears that he'd fool with fi-nancial records, cut her out of bank accounts or some-thing. That way, she figured she'd have an untouched version of their accounts." Flannery smiled at the expression on Matt's face. "I told you, she's not the most sophisticated person when it comes to computers."

"Sophisticated?" Matt echoed. "You'd have to work pretty hard to be that ignorant. Didn't she ever learn in school—"

"It was a different era," Flannery said. "A good school was one that had one computer per classroom."

Matt silently shook his head.

"Anyway," the priest went on, "Mrs. Knox asked me where she could get help sorting out what's in her former husband's computer. Family accounts, records—"

And maybe a few terabits of contraband information about a certain incident in Haddington, Matt silently finished. "Did you look?" he asked.

The priest shook his head, looking a little more uncomfortable. "I honestly told her that I'm not all that technically inclined." He hesitated, finally going on. "Then, I may have bent the truth a little. I reminded the widow of my first visit, with you, building you up as quite the computer wiz. Mrs. Knox is very eager to meet you again—for your professional opinion. Can you handle that?"

Matt smiled. "If I can't, I'll be sure to bring along someone who can."

As soon as Matt got home, he put out a call to his Net Force Explorers crew, inviting them in for a virtual meeting that evening. After dinner he whipped through his homework, then leaned back on his computer-link couch and synched in.

Matt entered his virtual work space, a black marble "desktop" floating unsupported in the midst of a starry sky.

One nice thing about veeyar, he thought, suddenly remembering Kerry Jones's dorm room. *You don't have to tidy it up when you have company.*

Leif Anderson popped into existence on the other side

of the desktop. "This is a nice setup," he said, folding his legs so that he was floating in a modified lotus position. He glanced down toward a distant galaxy. "Must be hard on people with acrophobia, though."

"I have a special sim for those visitors—it's a precise re-creation of the inside of my closet." Before Matt could say anything else, Megan was beside him. She ignored the stars, checking out the icons arranged on the desktop to spot any new programs she might want to borrow.

Megan was telling him he ought to upgrade his virtmail system when David Gray appeared.

"You're late!" She delighted in announcing to the usually punctual David. "That bum leg of yours is slowing you up even in veeyar!"

"It's not the bum leg, but the cane." David made an annoyed noise. "Especially when you have two younger brothers playing with it. I was stranded at the dinner table until my mother restored order."

Andy Moore appeared after that story, so he had no comments. And, since he was always late, nobody had a comment about that.

Matt waited until everyone was comfortably seated or sprawled in midair, then started talking. "Last night," he finished, "I had a meeting with the people—the few who are left of them—from the mystery sim I told you about. I wanted to get them up to date on some stuff I had learned, to keep the flow of information going."

"Better watch out with that line," Andy warned. "It sounds like the old hackers' motto: 'Information must be free!'"

Ignoring the comment, Matt went on, "I thought maybe we should do the same—you know, share information. If I run over stuff you've heard before, I apologize. I just want to make sure we're all on the same page."

His friends listened quietly while he summarized the case, paying special attention to what Captain Winters had said about the arson investigation, and what the sim participants had said when they'd gotten together.

"I've also got a piece of new business." Matt then re-counted his meeting with Father Flannery, going on to cover the Widow Knox and her disconnected computer.

"If she just unplugged it, she probably screwed up the operating system," Andy said. "Any flash memory would certainly be gone."

"But the long-term memory files should survive." As Matt hoped, David's eyes had a techie's gleam. The idea of reconstructing someone else's computer appealed to him.

"The widow is hoping for financial statements and family records," Matt said.

Andy snorted. "Which anybody with half a brain could get off the Net."

Matt leaned forward. "Knox was thrown out of the house. He didn't expect that. So there may be other stuff tucked away in the computer's fixed memory."

"You mean if he's the hacker who started all the trouble," Leif said.

"But the lawyers are still all over you and your sim-mates for hacking," Megan pointed out. "To me, that sounds like the hacking is still ongoing. So how can he be the hacker?"

"What?" Andy asked. "You think there's more than one?"

"I have no idea anymore," Matt admitted. "But I've got a chance to look in this guy's system legally—"

"Which is more than anybody else would give you," Andy cracked.

"And I've got the communications code for the Widow Knox and could give her a call. I could use some help." Matt turned to David. "That is, if you're willing to lend your technical expertise."

"We'll have to get at the computer physically," David said. "Maybe Saturday—"

"In the afternoon," Megan broke in. "I have a judo class in the morning."

Matt glanced at her.

"Oh, I'm going," she said before he could say anything. "This is something I want to see."

That was more help than Matt had counted on, but he saw he'd never win an argument with Megan. So he shrugged and said, "Okay. I'll make the call and see what happens. Does anyone have anything to add? Is there anything we're missing?"

Andy pointed to Matt's desktop. "You're missing a call right now."

The tiny, sculptured ear that represented Matt's virt-mail account was flashing with an urgent intensity.

"Not a call," Matt said. "A message." He reached down and activated the program. The display that popped into view was framed in flames—a visual metaphor for hot news.

Megan, typically, craned her head so she could read over Matt's shoulder. "Who's Dave Lowen?" she asked, frowning. "The name sounds familiar—"

"He's a character in the Lucullus Marten stories." Matt's frown was even deeper as he looked at the sender's name. "Marten uses the guy if Monty Newman is busy, or if the job requires a special finesse."

Megan gave a bark of laughter. "The message is addressed to Monty Newman. Whoever it is mustn't know you've retired."

"Oh, I think they know, all right," Matt said as he read the rest of the message.

Even Lucullus Marten never tried to solve a forty-year-old mystery. Here are a few points you might want to consider:
Who was the first officer on the scene?
How long did it take for Walter G. to be questioned?
When was his car impounded?
What happened to the car?

"I can tell you the answer to number one," Megan said. "So can Leif."

Leif nodded. "The cop was Clyde Finch, who went on to become head of the Callivants' personal security—and thanks to his seventeen-year-old daughter, also became Nikki Callivant's great-grandfather."

"Sounds like he could have done a better security job on his darling daughter," Andy cackled.

"Looking past that . . . you really have to question the guy's capacity for the job," David said. "The world is full of Secret Service and FBI alumni who would kill for a gig like guarding the Callivants. How does it wind up going to a small-town—"

"Flatfoot?" Andy suggested, earning a dirty look from the cop's son.

"I think we agree that Mr. Finch should be looked into," Matt said hurriedly. He glanced at Leif, who shrugged.

"I'll take a crack at it," he promised. "And I think I know the answer to the second question. From what I've read, Walter G. Callivant wasn't questioned until three days after the body was discovered. He'd suffered some sort of collapse and was in a sanitarium."

"Convenient," David snorted. "I bet the cops really took the gloves off—a rich kid surrounded by a phalanx of shrinks."

"Not to mention lawyers," Andy said.

"How about the next question?" Megan put in. "When did the cops get their hands on Walter G.'s car?"

"That I don't know," Leif admitted. "Although, according to what I've read, the police technicians gave it a clean bill of health when they finally saw it."

"After how many trips through the car wash?" Andy asked.

"The found no blood or tissue residues, and that sort of stuff is harder to wash away than you'd think," Leif said. "The medical examiners estimated that Priscilla Hadding had fallen—or was pushed—from a moving car. Her leg got hung up on something—probably the car door—and she was dragged for a bit."

Megan shuddered. "Ugly."

David nodded. "But it absolutely would have left traces of evidence on the car."

"So why is the question being asked?" Megan demanded. "Our new virtmail pal seems to think it's important."

" 'Deep Throat,' " Leif muttered.

She whirled on him. "What?"

"Just a name from another old scandal—but political instead of social this time. Somebody was troubled by the way an old President had gotten himself reelected and passed on some information to a couple of journalists. It worked. The president had to resign. And the reporter's nickname for the leak—'Deep Throat'—became a part of history."

"Well, our version of 'Deep Throat' would have to be pretty old to be troubled about something that happened forty years ago," Megan said.

"Maybe his conscience finally started getting to him," Andy suggested with a grin.

Leif shook his head. "More likely, this is the hacker, rubbing our noses in what he's found."

"Weren't we just saying that we thought Knox was the hacker?" David asked.

"Virtmail from beyond the grave," Andy said in a hollow voice.

"I don't know who this is, but he or she is certainly playing with us," Matt growled. "If two of those questions could be answered just by looking in books about the case—"

"How about the last one?" Megan cut in. "What *did* happen to Walter G.'s car?"

"It was a classic Corvette—1965," Leif said. "A lot of people were turning to older cars in the 1980s because government regulations were adding all sorts of antismog equipment to the new ones. It took awhile before the technology got good enough so that the power drain wasn't noticeable."

"What a terrible idea! Antismog devices!" Megan said sarcastically.

"It wasn't much fun at the time, if you wanted to drive a fast car," Matt said.

"Shouldn't be too hard to track down what happened to the Walter G.-mobile," Leif said. "All we need is the vehicle identification number—"

He shut up when he saw Matt shaking his head. "I may not know about scandals, but I do know about cars. The V.I.N. system didn't come into play until 1981. We won't be able to trace the car that way."

"That means a quiet visit to the dead files of the D.M.V.," Leif began, then cleared his throat. "Oops, I didn't say that. And nobody needs to hear about it from anybody in this room."

"No witnesses," David agreed.

"So we're batting .500 in the 'Deep Throat' trivia game," Andy said. "We had answers to about half of the questions."

"Your ear's blinking again," Megan announced.

Matt activated the program again. A similar message to the previous one appeared.

Since you picked up my first message so quickly, I suspect you're still linked in. Here's an additional clue.

As the kids watched, an image began to appear under the words. It was a reproduction of a faded flatfilm color photograph—a young man sitting behind the wheel of a low-slung antique car, grinning through the convertible's windshield.

"Computer!" Matt shouted. "Can you find the original source of that message?"

The computer displayed the name of a big and anonymous commercial remailing firm.

"Never mind, then. From the details available in the displayed image, can you project the make of the car?"

The computer was silent for a moment, then responded, "Probability, eighty percent or better."

"Then enlarge the image, restore the colors, and add the car."

Beneath the driver's smiling face, a quick procession of ghostly cars flickered into and out of view. Matt's hobby was virtual automobiles, and his computer had a vast collection of makes and models in its databases.

Finally the ghost car began to solidify. The faded colors grew more vibrant. The grinning young man now sat in a bright red sports car.

"Closest match—model 1965 Corvette Stingray," the computer announced.

"Callivant's car?" Andy asked. "Is that Callivant in the driver's seat?"

"No." Megan leaned forward. "Put on forty years of weight and wrinkles, take the hair away . . . and you've got Clyde Finch."

"Finch!" Leif took a harder look, then began to nod. "You're right. You know, we really do need to find out more about him."

"Maybe," Matt said. "But that's not the person who interests me right now."

"Who, then?" David asked.

Matt reached out as if he were trying to catch the image projected from the computer console. Of course, his fingers simply slipped through the hologram. "I want to know who the frack sent us this picture. Right now I have about as much chance of getting hold of him as I have of grabbing this image with my bare hands."

14

"Your problem," Leif Anderson told Matt, "is that you were thinking of the wrong tools. You don't capture images with your hands. You use a carefully targeted computer program."

"And you have a computer program that will catch Deep Throat for us?" Matt asked skeptically.

"I have one that will make a good try at tracing Deep Throat, if he or she virtmails you again," Leif replied. He didn't mention that the program would also alert him that such a trace was in progress.

In the end everybody had a job. Leif would get the tracing program to Matt—and it was unspoken but expected that he'd also try a raid on the D.M.V. records. Andy would take a whack at Clyde Finch and his background. Matt would get in touch with Mrs. Knox to arrange a look at her late husband's computer. And he, Megan, and David would do the looking on Saturday.

Leif cut his connection, returning to his own virtual workspace, an Icelandic stave house. Wind-driven snow howled past the windows, but Leif ignored the show outside. He went to a set of floor-to-ceiling shelves, shallow ones, broken up into small niches. Each open box held a program icon.

Reaching the center of the shelves, Leif searched for and found an icon that looked like the carving of a Chinese demon in a very bad mood. Rather than picking it up, Leif hooked a finger behind it and pulled. A whole section of shelving swung away, revealing a hidden set of niches set into the wall. This was Leif's combination treasure chest and armory. It held the tracking program he was going to lend Matt, and several tools that might make his visit to the Delaware Department of Motor Vehicles much simpler—and untraceable.

Leif's first choice was an icon shaped like a fishhook. That was the program that would catch on and leave a line to the mystery virtmailer. Then he got one that looked like a miniature hand at the end of a stick, another that looked like a tiny statue of Dracula peeking over his cape, and last, a tiny gold badge. That one was a last resort. It was supposed to contain police codes for demanding information. That would get Leif in real trouble if somebody found it in his possession.

However, he'd have to be caught first, and he'd do his best not to be. Closing the door on his secret hideout, he went to the living room couch. Composing a virtmail message for Matt, he gave an order, holding out the fishhook. A second later there were two in his hands. He put one down, sent off the message with another order, and the icon in his hand vanished.

That was the easy part of the job. Next Leif commanded his computer to contact the long-term record storage system of the Delaware state government. "Maximum confusion," he added, bracing himself.

The light show of the Net was hallucinatory enough when visitors traveled through it using their normal visualization techniques. Leif's "Maximum confusion" order implemented a program designed to frustrate any attempts to backtrack his visit to the state government's computers. To do that, the program bounced him at high speed from Net site to Net site to Net site, sending his connection randomly among millions of data and holographic transmissions. The experience was like participating in a really garish pinball game with a thousand paddles—as the ball.

Just when he thought he couldn't take it anymore, Leif's virtual journey ended—right outside yet another of those blank-sided boxes where old, computerized information went to die. Leif didn't want to try going in yet—if he had, his connection would have been tagged and recorded. Acting more on instinct than on any plan, Leif moseyed away from the front of the construct, heading around to the left side.

It was blank, of course—you weren't supposed to come in this way. Leif got out the hand-on-the-stick icon. It represented a universal handshaking program, which he now inserted into the glowing neon wall in front of him. It sank in, and then so did Leif. The plan was to blend in with any regular information traffic and make his way to the records he wanted.

Along the way Leif activated his vampire program, which was supposed to make him invisible and help him suck up any information he wanted.

Now came the difficult part. Would there be any protection for information relating to the Callivants? Leif could imagine guarding sealed court records. But forty-year-old car registrations? It seemed safe enough. Still, the body count on Matt's sim was getting awfully high—it might pay to be careful. And he'd hate to get caught hacking—it would get him booted out of the Net Force Explorers, at the very least.

The Callivant compound apparently was home to a fleet of cars at any given time. Tracking back through the old records, he came across a 1965 Corvette registered to Walter G. Callivant in 1981. Nothing in 1980. Nothing in 1982. No, wait—there was the transfer of registration—to Clyde Finch. A month later the car was junked.

That might explain the picture of Finch in the car, Leif thought. *But it raises another question. If you were the proud owner of such a hot set of wheels, happily photographed showing them off, why would you get rid of them?*

Friday afternoon came, and Matt felt pretty pleased with himself. He was still alive, and none of the other sim participants had had any trouble. He'd aced a history quiz this morning, and during lunch he'd made the necessary plans with Megan and David for their visit tomorrow with Mrs. Knox.

The widow had sounded pretty harassed when he called. She'd answered on her wallet-phone, but what Matt had mostly gotten was an earful of wailing baby. On hearing that he was calling for Father Flannery, however, the woman had nearly broken down herself.

"It would be such a help," Mrs. Knox said. "The bank won't do anything over the phone, and with two kids, it's hard to get down there. I don't like computers, but we really need the stuff that was trapped in there."

She eagerly agreed to having Matt and his friends over on Saturday afternoon. "You know where it is, right? I'll take the kids out so there'll be no distractions."

Most people would be more worried about having near-strangers alone in the house than about the noise level distracting those near-strangers, Matt thought. *I guess Mrs. K. figures we're already digging through all the family secrets in the computer, so she can trust us with the good china.*

If there was any in the house.

Matt pushed that downer of a thought away, determined to hold on to his good mood. Dismissal finally came, and he walked to the corner, ready to cross and wait for the autobus home.

A car pulled up at the intersection and honked at him.

It was the bronze Dodge concept car. The driver wore oversized sunglasses. This time, however, Nikki Callivant had a khaki cotton hat crammed down on her head.

The horn sounded again, and Nikki beckoned to him. Sighing, Matt went round to the passenger side and climbed in.

"Where to this time?" he asked. "The park again?"

"I thought I'd give you a lift home," Nikki Callivant said.

"How nice. Would it ruin the mood if I asked why?"

The girl slipped off her shades and gave him a look with those incredible blue eyes. "If you think it's because I can't keep my hands off you—you'd be very wrong."

"A lot of guys think that around you?" Matt asked.

"Too many," she said curtly. "Maybe it's a rich-guy thing."

"Yeah," Matt said. "I hear their feelings get hurt very easily. In fact, it happens with rich kids in general. Look at the way Priscilla Hadding stormed off on your grandfather, or vice versa."

"Have you found out any more about that?" It was lucky they'd stopped at a red light. Nikki was staring at his face instead of the road.

"If I found out anything, you'd be the last person I'd tell," Matt finally said.

A horn sounded behind them, and Nikki had to turn her attention back to traffic. "Why?" she asked as they started moving again.

"Flattered as I am by your attention, you're the enemy," Matt told her. "Your family is threatening me and everyone else connected with a dopey little mystery sim with nasty legal stuff for showing any interest whatsoever in what happened in Haddington forty years ago."

"More than forty years now," Nikki corrected. She sighed. "Why can't people let the past be?"

Matt bit his tongue to hold back the traditional P.I. answer—"There's no statute of limitations on murder."

"From what the senator—my great-grandfather—says,

the media people were actually a bit more decent back then. They still knew some shame and weren't quite as intrusive."

"Oh? News feeding frenzies weren't quite as frequent in the good old days?"

"It's easy for you to laugh. You don't spend half your life with your face in someone's viewfinder. As long as I can remember, I've had people poking at me, training me how to behave in public. Don't show too much emotion. Don't get into fights. Before you do anything, think how it would look to eighty million people seeing it on a holo display. I can't even go out on somebody's yacht without being shadowed by some cameraman in a boat or copter, his telephoto lens at the ready, just hoping I'll take off the top of my bathing suit."

"Must be awful, trying to get a tan."

"See? You just don't understand!"

"I understand this much about celebrity," Matt replied. "For fame, fortune, or public service—which is another way of saying power—people court public attention. They hire people to get them news coverage, they dream up publicity stunts. Then, when whatever they do is sure to be deemed newsworthy, they complain about the invasion of their privacy. If your name was Nikki McGillicuddy and you wanted to break into Hollywood, your manager would probably be telling you to drop the top of your bathing suit wherever you went."

Dull red glowed on the tops of Nikki's cheekbones. "I never asked—"

"No, previous generations have set up the publicity apparatus for you," Matt cut in. "But you're ready to use it—didn't I hear you talking about being the first female Callivant in the family power-brokering business?"

"You make it sound—I'm a Callivant!"

"And what's that?" Matt demanded. "A brand name in American politics? Somehow the republic got along for more than a hundred years before a Callivant appeared in Washington. Do you think civilization will collapse if one of your relatives isn't running things?"

"You dare—"

"Normally, I *wouldn't* dare to talk to a Callivant this way," Matt cut in. "The fact that you're letting me get away with it, throwing only a mild huff, makes me suspect you want something from me."

He stared at her finely chiseled profile while she kept her eyes on the road. "The problem is, I'm not all that sure what it is you want."

"I wanted to see why your friends went out of their way to help you," Nikki snapped. "What was there about you that inspired such loyalty?"

"And?"

"Frankly, I don't see it."

"Well, you know, we children of the lower classes get prickly when our betters take an interest in us," Matt said pointedly.

Nikki's voice got soft. "It's just that you were in trouble, and your friends—no one would do that for me."

"What are you talking about? You've got a house full of security guards to make sure trouble never comes close."

"Mercenaries," Nikki said bitterly. "They get fired if people think they're getting too close."

"It doesn't have to be that way." Matt thought of the stories Leif told about his father's chauffeur/security guy. Thor Hedvig had been almost as much of a father figure for Leif as Magnus Anderson. "Wait a minute," he said, "your great-grandfather is in charge of all those mercenaries."

"Grandpa Clyde." Nikki's voice was still soft, but there was a subtle shift . . . a hardening. "His loyalty is to the family—" her breath caught—"not to me."

However she'd learned that, it must have been a pretty severe lesson.

Nikki Callivant pulled over to the side of the road. "I wanted you to have this," she said, passing him a card with her name and a Net address. "I thought that maybe I could help you—or at least talk to you."

"Yeah," Matt said, ripping out a notebook page and scribbling his communications code. "Maybe it's a good idea if we kept in touch. At least this way, you won't have to honk at me."

That got a ghost of a smile from her. They sat in the parked car in silence for a while. For Matt, it was a weird feeling. He felt as if he'd really communicated with the rich girl at last, but they weren't saying anything.

Finally he said, "It's getting late, and you have a trip back to Haddington."

"Oh!" Nikki went to start the car.

Matt pointed to the next corner. "There's an autobus stop over there. That will take care of me. You head for home."

Moments later he stood at the stop, watching the bronze Dodge slide away into traffic.

She wants to help me, he thought, smiling. *But she can't even get me home.*

Leif sighed when he saw Andy Moore's face swim into being in his computer's display. Bad enough he was grounded and unable to go anywhere this Friday night. But being the target of one of Andy's pranks—or having to lend an ear to some of his awful jokes—that verged on cruel and unusual punishment.

Andy looked very satisfied with himself.

"What's up, Moore?" Leif said warily.

"I took care of my part," Andy reported.

"Your part of what?" Leif wanted to know.

"Clyde Finch. I was supposed to check him out, remember? That little meeting we had? You got the car? I got the guy? All I needed was a D.O.B., and that I managed to get from one of the books on the Callivants."

Leif nodded. With a date of birth, it would be easy enough to search for a birth certificate. And nowadays there weren't that many children being named Clyde.

Once he had a location, it wouldn't be too tough for Andy to find other Finches in the locality.

"So," he said, "is our boy one of the illustrious Delaware Finches?"

Andy shook his head. "Nope. He's a New Jersey Finch, born in a lovely town called Carterville. The main local business is a branch of the New Jersey Department of Corrections. Apparently, the Finch family took it as their mission to provide the place with inmates."

"Really?" Leif said. "That's a rather interesting background for a cop."

Grinning, Andy nodded. "Looks like Clyde's parents moved out of state to save the poor boy from evil influences. By the time he was fourteen, he had already had a few run-ins with the law. In one of them his sixteen-year-old cousin got nailed for car theft. The young genius didn't have his record sealed because he fought the case on one of those old flatscreen TV shows—*Everybody's Courtroom*. Ronnie Finch tried to blame everything on his cousin and lost."

"Any more on Clyde from Delaware records?" Leif asked.

"He seems to have cleaned up his act after his family moved to Haddington," Andy said. "Maybe he decided that if you couldn't beat the cops, you might as well join them."

"Maybe," Leif said, his mind already busy trying to see if the new piece of data fit with everything else he'd learned about Priscilla Hadding's death.

So that was no hick cop who was first to see the death scene, he thought. *Instead, we've got a pretty streetwise former punk who stumbles across a case involving rich, powerful people.*

And a couple of months later he was working for the Callivants and driving a classic muscle car. All the pieces might not yet fit together on that particular puzzle. But Leif already didn't like the picture he was seeing.

•   •   •

Megan wrinkled her nose. The Knox house smelled of baby food and used diapers, perhaps only to be expected with two really little kids on the premises. *In one end, and out the other,* she thought.

The place was so small that a smell in any room was soon shared with the others. At least the kids were out. Mrs. Knox had met them at the door with a double-barreled stroller. She'd shown them the computer and bailed, saying she'd be back in a couple of hours. Megan, Matt, and David went into the postage-stamp living room. A swaybacked sofa faced a dedicated holo unit. Squashed in the corner was Harry Knox's computer console and a worn but good quality computer-link couch.

David frowned as he looked over the hardware. "This looks like a pretty ancient system. If he was trying to hack his way into anything using this junk, it's a wonder he wasn't caught on his first try." He pointed. "It's like a first-generation Net system, with a docking port for old-style laptops." Then he looked harder. "Huh. The external adapters have been changed to accommodate machines like this." He pulled out his own laptop computer, a last shot at the technology devised and marketed by Anderson Investments Multinational. The failure to generate a market had resulted in bargain prices for many Net Force Explorers.

"Maybe Knox didn't have the money for a brand-new computer system after he got his truck," Megan suggested. "So he bought himself a laptop and adapted an older model."

David had already removed the console's front panel. "Yeah," he said. "We've got ourselves a hobbyist here. All sorts of circuit boards, different makes and models—aftermarket stuff."

"These were on the kitchen counter where Mrs. Knox said they'd be," Matt said, offering a double handful of crumpled papers. "Whenever her husband changed the passwords, she'd write them down on scratch pad sheets and stick them in a drawer."

"Great security," Megan muttered, glancing over some of the scrawled notations: Icarus287, WILDEYEZ. "Would have been better if she'd put dates on them."

David continued to poke around in the guts of the system. "This may be more straightforward that I thought," he said. "I'll power this sucker up, hook in my laptop, and boot from that."

With the system up and running, he began running through Mrs. K.'s collection of passwords. A couple of them actually worked, letting him into some of the data areas.

After that the job was to get into the areas that were still marked with virtual "no trespassing" signs. But David had programs to crack his way in—some of them donated by Leif Anderson.

"How's it going?" Megan asked, watching a hail of strange characters scroll down the system's holographic display.

"This stuff is encrypted, so I'm just piping it into my laptop," he said. "Decoding it is going to take some time—but I bet I'll be able to crack it on my system back home."

David gestured to the computer in front of them. "Nothing in here is what you'd call cutting edge." He grinned. "I'm betting it will be the same with his security."

"If Hard-Knocks Harry's system is so rickety, how did he get away with his hacking?" Matt asked.

"Two words come to mind," David said. "Sheer luck." He pointed again at the hodgepodge of circuits. "I think that when he cobbled this together it gave Mr. Knox a totally unfounded sense of confidence—he began branching out."

"Until he began jangling somebody's alarms. Hey!" Megan said, pointing to the display. "Now we're getting pictures."

David took a squint at the title of the file. "Oh, yeah. The Cowper's Bluff Nature Preserve of Chesapeake Bay.

There's a whole bunch of files about this place. This is a public promo."

Megan frowned. "Was he thinking of taking a vacation there?"

David shook his head. "Almost nobody gets in. It's a wildlife sanctuary."

"But he has a bunch of files about it." Matt repeated. "I hope you're getting copies."

"If I copy them, the question will be what *don't* we take," David complained. "This guy stored data the way squirrels store nuts. He's got stuff from public-access Net sites—everything from P.R. handouts to nonsensical conspiracy theories, jumbled in cheek by jowl with encrypted data he stole but couldn't translate. And stuck in between, like raisins in an oatmeal cookie, nuggets of court records, police memos, and who knows what else?"

By the time Mrs. Knox and the kids turned up—two and a half hours later—Megan and her friends had printed out the records and saved them to datascrips, as well as putting the home system back online, and the family financial records in a format that made sense.

They also had their laptop computer and a bunch of datascrips filled with as much of Harry Knox's mishmash of data and misinformation as seemed relevant—and in David's opinion, a lot that wasn't.

Mrs. Knox had tears of gratitude in her eyes as they left. Megan felt an uncomfortable mix of emotions. On the one side, she was sorry for a woman who found herself in such a terrible position. But how could the woman live in such—such ignorance? And how had she let herself get in that position, where both she and her children were at risk because of technology she didn't understand?

Megan didn't say a word all the way to the autobus stop.

They had a bit of a wait—the Saturday schedule was much more limited than on weekdays. Even though the automated vehicles didn't require drivers, they did need maintenance. Most of it was taken care of on weekends.

At last the right autobus came up. They were all ready with their universal credit cards to flag the vehicle down, slipping them in the slot by the entrance door to pay their fare.

The autobus was empty—again, not a surprise. This wasn't a route that led to a mall or amusement center, so Saturday afternoon ridership would be sparse.

"Well, we've got our pick of seats," Megan said, moving along the bus aisle. She waited till David picked a seat, dropping into the one behind him. Matt chose the seat in front. It was the sunnier side of the bus, offering a little more watery, winter sunlight.

As Megan expected, David fired up his laptop as soon as he was seated. "I still think we've got the equivalent of Hard-Knocks Harry's junk-mail file," he complained, bringing up another view of the bird sanctuary. It showed a reedy inlet as seen from the top of a hill or cliff overlooking an expanse of water.

"There's nothing to connect birdland here with the Callivants," David went on.

Matt shook his head. "The preserve is on the Chesapeake. Where?"

David brought up some flowery text.

"There," Megan said, pointing at a map. "It's in Maryland."

Matt, however, pointed to another part of the display. "But the foundation that supports it is headquartered in Delaware. What a surprise! Haddington, Delaware."

"Silly me," David grumped. "Of course! This is where they buried the body. But wait! The body wasn't buried. It was found—about forty years ago!"

Megan looked out the window to ignore David's sarcasm. That's why she saw the black car with tinted windows that pulled up beside them—so close, it almost sideswiped the autobus. The rear window was open, but she didn't see a face. Instead, Megan saw a pair of hands—actually a pair of shiny black gloves—holding up a complicated-looking metal grid. Some sort of antenna assembly?

"Whoa!" Matt called out as the autobus swerved slightly, trying to maintain a safe distance from the car. "Crazy drivers—" he began.

His words were cut off by the sudden scream of the autobus's turbine engine. The vehicle lurched ahead, pressing Megan and her friends back against their seats while it cut off a car to the right.

These buggies aren't supposed to do that, Megan thought in surprise. *And they're certainly not supposed to go this fast. What—?*

Matt took the words right out of her brain. "What the frack is going on?" he shouted.

15

How many times, running a bit behind schedule, had Matt sat in an autobus seat, alternating anxious glances at his watch with silent curses at the vehicle's maddeningly slow speed? The metropolitan autobus system had a national reputation for dependability, safety ... and a speed that made turtles look swift in comparison.

Just my luck, Matt thought as he clutched for the metal handle on the seat in front of him. *Now I wind up on the one autobus trying out for the stock-car racing circuit!*

The autobus was careening madly along the six-lane boulevard, muscling other vehicles out of the way as if it suddenly believed it was a stock car. So far the bus was maintaining its programmed route, but even as Matt watched, the bus roared past a stop where people had been attempting to flag it down.

What are they, nuts? he wondered. *This thing's clearly not doing what it's programmed to do!*

If anything, the computer running the bus seemed to be increasing its road rage. Brakes squealed and horns uselessly sounded as the vehicle cut through traffic even more aggressively. Then came a screech that put Matt's teeth on edge. Metal against metal—a car scraping its way along the side of the bus. The impact sent the bus shuddering up on two wheels. And when it bounced down, Matt and his friends had to fight to keep from flying.

That left David at a disability—he had too much stuff to hang on to. The bump left his cane skittering one way while his laptop took off in another. David, of course, went to rescue his computer, reaching out with both hands.

Right then the autobus jarred its way through a lane change. Matt and Megan were just jostled. David caught his computer, but he didn't have a grip on anything to hold himself in place. He went tumbling from his seat, still clutching the laptop.

Matt launched himself into the aisle, one hand clenched on the tubular seat grip, the other outstretched to snag David's arm as he hurtled by.

The good news was that Matt managed to catch David. The bad news was that the autobus lurched round on a new tack, spinning both boys around in the aisle.

David didn't cry out, but Matt heard a wheeze of pain hiss from between his friend's clenched teeth as he landed on his bad leg. Then Matt wasn't hearing much of anything. The edge of his forehead smashed against a pole set in the aisle. It was supposed to offer a grip for standees during rush hour. But for someone flailing around in a near-empty bus, it was a disaster.

Bright yellow novas of pain erupted in the back of Matt's eyeballs. He lost his hold, and both he and David went skittering along the thrumming floor to the rear of the autobus.

Matt's cheek felt wet. *Oh, man,* he thought, *have I landed face-first in somebody else's mess?*

As he came to rest in the back of the bus, he tried to wipe off whatever was on his face. But the barest touch sent a new twinge of pain though him. His fingers smeared some slimy/sticky gunk across his skin.

"Matt!" David's voice sounded oddly far away. "Are you all right?"

" 'M *I* awri?" Matt slurred. "Howze ya leg?"

"Bad," David gritted. "How's your face?"

"Face?" Matt blinked his eyes, trying to get them to focus. He wasn't seeing stars anymore. Now he could make out David's concerned face leaning over him.

Matt raised his hand. Now he could see what the slimy/sticky stuff was. Blood.

His blood.

Matt tried to rise up from his prone position, but either the sudden movement was too much for him . . . or maybe the crazed bus had just whirled end for end. He thumped back, trying hard not to throw up.

"Easy—easy!" David said.

Matt tried standing up again, much more slowly this time. His attempt to turn was more like a flop. But he managed to lever himself up, first on his elbows, then on his hands, until he was halfway into a push-up position. He was also wondering who was sitting on his shoulders.

David grabbed him as the bus wildly shimmied through another lane change. "I think you just split the skin where you hit," he told Matt, looking closely at his forehead. "But it's bleeding like a sonova—"

"Frack!" Megan's shout from the front of the bus drowned out David's words. "Stupid fracking hammer! Where is it?"

While David and Matt had been bowled to the back of the autobus, she'd fought her way to the front—and the emergency cutoff switch. This was supposed to stop the bus dead in its tracks. Every kid who rode an autobus had it drummed into his or her head that this button was to be touched only in the direst emergencies.

Well, that's what this is, Matt thought as he tried to see what Megan was doing up there. His right eye—the one under the cut on his head—seemed to have its lids gummed together somehow. Matt couldn't quite see—

Wait—Megan was pounding with her fist on the transparent plastic plate that protected the cutoff button. What was she doing that for? There was supposed to be a little metal hammer chained in place—

Oh. *That's* what she'd been swearing about. The hammer wasn't there. And the button couldn't be pushed until she got the protective plate out of the way.

Matt's head sank back to the floor. He noticed a grinding noise entering the whine of the autobus engine. Of course, the motor wasn't built to power the kind of high-speed maneuvers the vehicle's out-of-control computer was attempting. It might just blow a valve or something and they'd end up rolling to a stop. On the other hand, the engine might blow or start a fire, and they'd be trapped in a fast-moving inferno. Or they might stop by crashing into something—maybe even killing all of them plus some innocent bystanders. Megan had to get to that button—now!

He looked around for something to use as a tool—and his hand fell on David's cane.

"Megan! Here!" Matt tried to toss the cane underhand. His arm didn't move as well as he wanted it to, and the cane clattered to the floor about four feet short of Megan's waiting hand. Luckily, momentum made the cane skid another foot or so, and Megan was able to stretch out a leg and catch the handle under her foot. Holding on to a pole by the entrance door, she crouched down, pulling the cane in with her foot while reaching with her free hand.

She grabbed on to the shaft of the cane and rose to both feet. With a yell she swung the cane handle against the protective window. It didn't break.

"What the—" Megan snarled, smacking the supposedly brittle plastic again—and again.

As if it knew what Megan was trying to do, the autobus began jinking back and forth from lane to lane. Megan was tossed one way, then the other, clinging despcrately to the pole. The bus doors opened. If the vehicle succeeded in throwing Megan loose, she'd become a smear on the pavement.

"Megan, get away from there!" David called.

Megan glanced over her shoulder. Even from a distance and with one decently working eye, Matt recognized the stubborn jut of her jaw. She braced both feet against the autobus dashboard, pressing her back into the pole. Then, using both arms, she brought the cane down on the clear barrier. It finally broke.

The bus careened again, and Megan lost the cane out the doorway. But somehow she managed to hold on to that pole. Regaining her balance, she launched a martial-arts high kick, nailing the emergency stop button squarely with her toe.

"Way to go, Megan!" Matt cheered.

The only problem was, the bus still wasn't stopping. Megan punched the button again, and again. The bus wobbled, but it didn't stop. The mutinous computer was apparently fighting the cutoff order. Now the ominous smell of frying circuit boards up front joined the increasingly scary engine noises in the rear.

"Megan, get away from there!" David pleaded.

"Why? So I can put myself into the best position to get hit when the turbine throws a vane?" Megan shouted back. She glared around the autobus interior like an Amazon searching for a weapon. "You guys get up here. These passenger poles are only screwed in place. We could work one loose and ram it into the computer housing. That should kill it."

And maybe us, too, with who knows how much electricity coming up the metal rod, Matt thought. *But it beats dying in a crash and taking out the whole bunch of us and anybody in the way.*

"Megan! Come back! We'll meet you in the middle!" he called. Maybe Megan's cutoff attempt had enjoyed some success. The autobus changed course again, this time veering to the right across the boulevard traffic. It didn't seem to be an attempt to self-destruct—at least the autobus wasn't aiming for a building. Bare trees, bushes, and bleached winter grass showed through the windows. They were heading into a park.

Not wanting to meet a tree trunk firsthand while moving at near light speed, Megan began making her way back from the front window. Matt and David struggled painfully to meet her halfway. David was crawling along the floor, his injured leg trailing behind him. Matt wasn't all that much better. He felt dizzy whenever he tried to raise himself higher than his knees.

The three friends met just as the bus jumped a curb.

"Hold tight!" Megan yelled, wrapping both arms around a pole.

The front tire bumped onto the sidewalk, turning the autobus at a steeper angle. Ahead was a steel-rod fence. They tore through as if it weren't there.

"I think we're slowing down a little," Megan said, peering out the window. Matt and David were both too low to see anything but tree branches whipping past.

"Probably because the dirt under this grass is soaked from snow melt and rain," David said. "Pure mud."

"I think we're going slightly uphill, too," Matt added.

"We're still going too fast to try a jump." Megan's face reflected her obvious thought. *Especially with the two of you so badly banged up.*

Matt pulled himself into a position where he could see through the front windshield. The bus plowed its way through a planting of brush. Then came a clear area, and—

"This may be it!" he yelled. "We've got a tree coming up at one o'clock!"

The autobus was still moving at an angle and might have made it past the large, old oak with only a body scrape. But the right front wheel hit a boggy spot, and the whole bus sheered around as it pushed its way out. In the windshield, the tree moved from well to the right to dead center, then slightly to the left.

Megan dropped down to Matt and David's level. "We're not going to miss," she said. "Hold on tight!"

They all climbed between seats in the back, bracing themselves as best they could.

Matt closed his eyes.

The autobus hit the tree with a bone-shaking crash! Then the front windshield shattered, sending shards of glass tinkling all over the place. The bus heeled round as if some giant had punched it in the face. It bounced free, the engine noise rising to a shriek as the wheels revved in thin air. The suspension screamed in protest. Only half the wheels—the ones on the right side—touched the ground.

Like a dog going to lie down, the autobus swung round in a half-circle. Then it overbalanced and toppled over on its side.

Matt and his friends rode out the impact as best they could. The wheels were still spinning mindlessly in the air as Megan pushed her way to the bus windows that were now overhead. She grabbed the red emergency handle on them, pulled, then pushed against the frame. The window flew up on a hinge and fell over.

Megan climbed out, then leaned back inside. "Help David get up!" she shouted.

Though still wobbly on his own feet, Matt managed to get David upright. His friend still clung to his laptop computer.

"Let me hold it," Matt said. "You're gonna need both hands to get out of here."

"I'm not leaving without that sucker," David vowed.

"I'll hand it up before I even try climbing," Matt said. "Promise."

With Matt pushing from below and Megan hauling from on high, they managed to get David out the window. David held Matt to his promise. Matt had to hand up the laptop computer before he began climbing.

Then it was his turn to climb to freedom. For one awful second, his legs buckled. He didn't think he was going to make it. Two sets of arms grabbed him, holding him in place until he managed to catch a foothold. He made it! He was out!

From there it was a simple job to get away from the crazed autobus. Matt and David helped Megan transfer to the ground. She controlled David's descent as Matt lowered him into Megan's arms. Finally Matt slithered down the roof of the bus while his friends tried to catch him.

Then, with Megan bracing David on his bad side and Matt hanging on to the other shoulder, they staggered away from the still-screaming bus.

We probably look like we just lost a war, Matt thought. *But this feels like a victory to me.*

They made it through the newly torn hole in the bushes when Matt heard oncoming sirens. Megan stumbled, and the three of them went down.

With luck, they were far enough away to survive if the autobus decided to explode.

Matt hoped.

Megan was leaning against the tailgate of the Emergency Services ambulance, watching the paramedics patch David and Matt, when a familiar face passed her field of vision.

"Captain Winters!" she called out in surprise.

Winters wheeled on hearing her voice and came straight over. "I came here as soon as I heard the names of the passengers on that bus." His face filled with concern as he looked into the ambulance.

He probably did the same thing with his Marines, Megan thought. *Taking care of his men. Once a military man, always a military man.*

"The kids all came through this surprisingly well," the paramedic stanching Matt's bleeding forehead assured the captain. "I've got the worst of them, and there's no signs of concussion here, although we'll have to check and make sure later. Otherwise, a few butterfly clips to close the wound, and the boy should be fine."

"We'll need an X ray to make sure that this young man's bone hasn't broken again," the young woman setting the pressure cast around David's leg said. "But I think it's fine, just bruised."

"I lost my cane in all the excitement," David said. He held his laptop computer cradled in his arms.

"I will personally see that you get a replacement cane," Winters promised. "What I'd like to hear now is—what in the world happened on that bus?"

"It went nuts," David said.

"Tried to break the land speed record back to my house," Matt put in. "When the on-board computer saw that wasn't going to happen, it apparently tried to take a short cut through the park."

"Another accident," Winters said grimly.

"Nuh-uh," Megan told him, remembering what happened right before the bus went haywire. "I don't think so. We were rolling along, just another boring Saturday ride, when this car came up beside the bus. I thought we were going to get sideswiped, but someone in the back of the car had a gizmo."

Winters leaned forward. "What kind of gizmo?"

"I only got a quick glance. It looked like some sort of flat antenna grid. That's all I saw—except it was shoved out at the front of the autobus."

"At the front—where the computers are. I've heard of experiments being done—the effects of a localized electromagnetic pulse—" Winters's eyes grew sharp. "Did you see anything to identify the car? The make? A look at the license plate?"

"It was black and had dark tinted windows, so I couldn't see anybody inside it. Sorry. What can I say?" Megan spread her hands. "That's when things began to get a bit exciting."

"Oh, yeah," Matt agreed. "The computer said, 'Wahoo! We're off to the races.' "

The captain pulled out his wallet-phone. "We have a

technical crew down here, and there's a team coming from the manufacturers. They expect to see some sort of accident. I'm going to pass along what Megan saw. Let's see if they find any—"

"Evidence," Matt finished for him. His pale face had a stony expression. "Otherwise, this *will* be just another accident."

"It might also explain one of the earlier ones," David said slowly. "What if the truck Harry Knox was driving got a taste of EMP? There's so much drive-by-wire control circuitry in those big rigs, it could have gone wild."

"And who'd really notice after the electronics took a nice dunk in the Potomac?" Megan added.

"Interesting question," Winters said, punching a code into his wallet-phone. Apparently it was to the central offices of Net Force, which in turn routed him to the tech crew at the wreck. The captain sketched out what Megan had seen, listened for a moment, then said, "Yes, we're at the ambulance."

A few minutes later they were joined by a short, balding guy with a big nose and glasses—he looked like a geek, not a Net Force agent.

Megan found herself wondering how the guy ever survived the combined FBI-Marine physical training course for Net Force officers. When he turned cold gray eyes on her, she began to suspect how.

"You saw some sort of aerial?" the man barked.

"It was flat, like a grid," Megan said. "Whoever was holding it needed both hands to keep it steady. I could draw it for you if that would help."

"Later," he said.

She closed her eyes, trying to reenvision the moment. Another detail came. "The person holding it had gloves on. Shiny gloves. Not leather. Something like—rubber? Plastic? Maybe for insulation?"

The technical guy made a disparaging noise and turned to Winters. "I don't know how much we'll be able to recover from the vehicle. Most of the circuit boards were damaged by the impact with the tree. Others had already burned out. Someone had activated the emergency cut-off." He made it sound like an accusation.

"Well, excuse me for trying to save our lives!" Megan flared. "That vehicle was doing something like ninety on the straightaways when it wasn't playing bumper cars with everything else on the road. If you don't believe us, check with Metropolitan Transit. I'm sure you'll find that we got here well ahead of schedule. Or you can check with all the motorists who almost got nailed, traffic control, and I'll bet we passed enough building security cameras to give you quite a show! Besides, the stupid cutoff button didn't work. We wobbled a bit, but we kept going."

"Is that the usual effect of an emergency cutoff?" Winters asked. "I always expected it to bring a bus to an instant stop—at least as instant as the brakes and the occupants could handle."

"What happened here was definitely anomalous," the techie said stiffly. "But, given the state of the hardware, I'm not sure we'll ever identify the exact nature of the failure."

He gave Megan an affronted look—an expert faced with an impertinent layperson.

The little guy was surprised when Matt's sarcastic voice rang out from the ambulance. "Sure, pal. Some failure! One that caused a *nearly* fatal accident."

16

On Monday afternoon the stream of students coming out of Bradford Academy generally moved quickly—happy to escape the first day of the school week. Matt Hunter was at the tail end of the rush. While he was glad that classes were over, he wasn't exactly eager to face another ride on an autobus.

Physically he was okay. The cut on his head was bandaged, and had developed a Technicolor bruise that pained him whenever he touched it. The good news was that David hadn't broken his leg again. David's recovery was still on track, and he now had a much fancier cane, courtesy of Captain Winters.

While the media had kept the kids' names out of the fairly sensational story of the autobus run amok, the Bradford rumor mill had been working overtime. According to the rumors, not only had Matt, Megan, and David been passengers on the mad bus, but apparently they were supposedly responsible somehow for the disaster. If the questions he was hearing were any guide, the kids at school thought they had somehow reprogrammed the bus into believing it was a race car. They also seemed to think that doing so was really, really cool. Nobody seemed to realize how close to getting killed they'd come—or to be able to explain why something that *stupid* would be cool.

Matt had kept his own opinions away from his new fan club—that anybody who tried that experiment while riding the bus *deserved* a broken head for their efforts. The only thing he regretted was that none of his new friends had offered him a lift home.

On the other hand, who'd want a ride from someone who admired people who destroyed safety interlocks?

Matt's mother had given him a lift to school this morning. But now Matt had to face the autobus alone.

It's just like the guys at the rodeo, he told himself. *You've got to get back on the horse that threw you.*

That didn't quiet the little voice in the back of his head that whispered, *What if another car comes by with one of those trick antennas?*

The thought of going through the same adventure, this time on a bus jammed with students, made him shudder. On the other hand, waiting for an empty bus didn't seem like the answer, either.

What I really need, he thought, *is for Nikki Callivant to come by and—*

His thoughts were interrupted by the beep of a car horn. Matt turned to see the now-familiar bronze car. Behind the wheel, Nikki Callivant had reduced her disguise to a baseball cap and sunglasses.

She pushed the shades up on her forehead to get a good look at him. "What happened to you?" she asked.

Matt came around and got in the passenger door. "Did you hear about the suburban autobus that went on the fritz? I was riding it. Quite a coincidence, huh?"

Nikki took her glasses off to stare at him. "I saw that on the news. What—"

"Here's something that never made the evening report. I was riding home with two friends. We'd spend the afternoon poking around in a computer that belonged to Harry Knox. You remember Hard-Knocks Harry? The truck driver whose big rig decided to take a dive?"

The rich girl continued to stare.

"By the way, I think he's the one your family had the problem with. He must have obsessed on you Callivants. Had all sorts of crap he'd gotten off the Net—in addition to material he must have hacked."

"And now you have it—?"

"No, we've spread it out as much as we could," Matt told her. "It seemed a little safer that way."

"Safer," she repeated, sounding almost dazed.

"I'll share one of the less earth-shaking tidbits he collected," Matt went on. "What does the Cowper's Bluff Nature Preserve mean to you?"

Nikki blinked. "It's a—well, it's a major Callivant cause. The Senator—my great-grandfather—started it. Years ago he saw the way things were going with the Chesapeake Bay. He bought some shoreland that was little more than a dump, fenced it off, and started the preserve. He used our family prestige to recruit other wealthy contributors. Some have even donated adjoining parcels of land. Now the preserve is a major bird sanctuary."

She spread her hands. "It's one of the reasons I was at the Junior League event where I met your friend Megan. Quite a few socially prominent families support Cowper's Bluff."

"How nice for the birds," Matt said.

"Why would that man have anything about the preserve in his computer?" Nikki asked.

"You've got me there," Matt admitted. "But he had all sorts of stuff. Publicity. Maps. Pictures. We were looking at them on the autobus—before things got exciting."

"What—" She stopped to swallow. "What happened?"

"The unofficial version?" Matt asked. "We think somebody came up in a car and scrambled the bus's electronic brains. Net Force is looking into it."

"Net Force?"

"Anything weird that happens with computers brings Net Force in," he explained. "Even if you might expect the National Transportation Safety Administration instead."

"How did you manage to keep the media people away?" Nikki asked.

"Easy," Matt replied. "We're not Callivants, and we're underage. The underage part is also good for court records. You can ask your grandfather about that."

A faint reddish tinge crept onto her cheeks when she heard that. But Nikki shrugged and started the car. "I guess you'd be glad of a lift all the way home this time," she said. Then, touching on Matt's last verbal dart, "I think Grandpa Clyde could talk more about youthful offenses." Nikki managed a grin. "To listen to him, he had a pretty colorful time growing up."

Matt shook his head. "Maybe it's because I've been reading too many detective novels lately," he said. "But you make Clyde Finch sound like the Great Detective's butler—the reformed safecracker."

Nikki's grin faded. "What do you mean?"

"I hear how you speak about the Callivant side of your family. Your great-grandfather is still the Senator, capital S. And Walter G. is Grandfather. But when it comes to Grandpa Clyde—you sound more like you're talking about a servant than a relative."

A full flush came to Nikki's cheeks. "You mean I'm a snob? Maybe. But so is Grandpa Clyde, in his own way. He told me years ago, 'Every family has its in-laws and its outlaws. I know where I fit—I'm definitely the Callivant outlaw.' "

She glanced over at Matt. "He was never going to fit into society. My grandmother Marcia kept at it, and she's a Callivant now."

"You make it sound like a disease," Matt said. " 'Can-she-ever-be-cured' kind of stuff."

Nikki Callivant sat very straight behind the wheel.

"Now you're just being insulting," she said.

"Okay, I'll apologize for that," Matt said. "But you haven't answered my question. Is Clyde Finch family or just a servant?"

She was silent for a long moment. "I guess he's the closest thing we've got to an old family retainer," Nikki finally replied. "Servants never stay. Never have. We weren't encouraged to get—personal—with them. When I got too attached to a nanny, she was replaced. But Grandpa Clyde was always around. A lot of the time he seemed to be the only non-Callivant I could talk to."

"But how did you *feel* about him?" Matt pressed.

Nikki Callivant didn't look at him, keeping her eyes on the road. "Maybe—maybe I looked down on him. But I also envied him. He wasn't a Callivant. He was free. Not a captive, like me."

After that, except for a few brief directions offered by Matt, they drove in silence.

Leif was working on some programmed classwork when the display on his computer suddenly went blank— everything saved and shelved. The audio cue that sounded—a shrill "peep-peep-peep!"—told him what was going on. The program he'd given to Matt had initiated a trace. Now it was sending to Leif to see if he wanted to join the hunt.

He gave his computer a few orders, adding its resources to the tracing job. That was just machine versus machine, anyway—trying to backtrack along the message's programmed zigzags through the Net. No need for a human brain to get involved yet.

Using the trace program's connection like a backdoor into Matt's system, Leif went into the virtmail files. There it was—another message from "Dave Lowen." Unless Andy Moore was trying some stupid prank, this had to come from the mysterious Deep Throat.

Working together, Matt and Leif's computers ground along the virtmail message's back trail. As he watched their progress along the twisty course, Leif found it reminded him of someone—

With a shock, he realized who that someone was—himself. The way the message bounced at high speed through heavily trafficked Net sites—the way it tried to camouflage itself within that traffic—he was looking at a near-copy of his Maximum Confusion program. And while Leif had tweaked it with a couple of additions he found useful, he hadn't created it. He wasn't a hacker, and neither, it seemed, was Deep Throat.

Maximum Confusion had cost him enough when he bought it from one of his less shadowy hacker contacts. By extension, the person he was looking for was probably a rich kid who liked to play on the Net. That knowledge was useful when the computers began having trouble figuring out some of the message's wilder hops. Understanding how he'd tweaked the program helped him work back for a couple of more bounces—in fact, right to the point where the message had originated.

Unfortunately, that turned out to be a remote location, an empty suite in a no-name virtual office building. Again, that was a rich person's response to maintain anonymity, actually renting a space. A real hacker could have wormed his way into a corporate address to download his naughty pictures, launch flame-mail attacks on rivals . . . or post virtmail messages to stir up the receiver without letting him know who the sender might be.

Okay, Leif told himself. *Do we know of anyone with more money than sense who might be obsessed with the Callivants and the death of Priscilla Hadding in particular?*

He was glad he didn't have to raise the question with his Net Force Explorer friends. Megan O'Malley would have had an immediate answer—"Leif Anderson!"

Was he missing some obvious connection? Who had brought him into contact with Nikki Callivant, in Haddington of all places, with even the late Priscilla's mother in attendance?

I always figured Charlie Dysart for the rich-and-brainless category, Leif thought. *Maybe I'll have to reconsider. The guy might be more subtle than I ever suspected.*

Doubling back on his failed trace, Leif reentered Matt's computer. He'd only made sure that the virtmail posting came from Deep Throat. This time he'd read what the mystery meddler had to say.

The body of the message was a simple police report from forty-four years ago. Some hacking skills had probably been necessary to get it—much as Leif had abstracted information from the defunct files of the Delaware D.M.V.

What was the big deal with a New Jersey State Police bulletin? Leif read on. Apparently a classic car had been stolen in the town of Rising Hills—a red Corvette Stingray, 1965 model.

Leif checked the date. It was the day after Priscilla Hadding's body had been found.

All of a sudden Leif remembered his last conversation with Andy Moore.

I wonder, he thought, *how far Carterville is from Rising Hills?*

Matt frowned at the split display floating over his computer. The moment he'd come home, his system had told him to call Leif. Now Leif's face took up the left-hand side of the display while the State Police report occupied the right.

The latest Deep Throat virtmail, even though the trace had petered out, offered serious food for thought. Matt was also annoyed that Leif had used the program he'd lent to get into Matt's computer.

"It's not as though I went on the unguided tour," Leif said, beginning to sound annoyed. "I didn't paw through your collection of bimbo-rock singers posing in swimsuits." He grinned. "Or without."

That was almost enough to make Matt check a few

files, but he held back. "I don't like people in my system—period," he said.

Leif sighed. "Fine. Point made. But I thought it just might be an emergency—the way this case is going, the sooner we solve it, the sooner we're all out of danger. So read your message. I'll talk to you later." He cut the connection.

Matt read the police report. Then he called up Andy Moore's virtmail describing the life and times of young Clyde Finch, scowling as he winnowed the facts from between Andy's wisecracks and self-congratulatory comments.

Finally Matt commanded his computer to project a map of New Jersey. "Locate Rising Hills," he commanded. Then, "Locate Carterville." He squinted as two red dots appeared on the map—quite close together. "Give me the distance between the two townships."

"Distance approximately 13.72 miles," the computer's silver-toned voice replied.

Matt sat in silence, his eyes staring unfocused at the map. A real-life noir mystery story was playing itself out inside his head. Once upon a time, back in 1982, a rich girl died in Haddington, Delaware. First on the scene was a smart cop with a shady past. It took three days for investigators to get to the young man most likely to be connected with the girl's death—and to get their hands on his car.

Meanwhile, just one day after the incident and three states away, an identical car disappears—where? Right near the clever cop's old hometown, where he apparently has lots of car-thief connections. These were the days before people got fanatical about part serial numbers. With a change of license plates, the clean but stolen Corvette could become Walter Callivant's car.

Add it all together, and what have you got?

For one thing, you'd have an explanation as to why the Callivants took on Clyde Finch as part of their security setup. He'd neatly packaged things so that an unpleasant scandal didn't turn into a nasty court case.

Fast-forward about forty-odd years. Some person or persons unknown (aka Harry Knox) starts setting off alarms around the records dealing with Priscilla Hadding's suspicious death.

Clyde Finch sees his work unraveling. What's the worst-case scenario? More scandal for the Callivants. Finch losing his cushy job. Legal repercussions? He's probably well past the statute of limitations for evidence tampering. But . . . if Walter G. Callivant turned out to be a murderer, there were no statutory limitations on that crime. He could still be tried for it. And Clyde Finch could be an accessory after the fact.

Matt blinked. It made an interesting story. Vivid characters, a couple of plot twists, conspiracy theory . . . there was even a little gore, if you threw in the "accidents" claiming the mystery gamers' lives.

Unfortunately, Matt didn't know the ending. And all he had was a wild bunch of theories with no actual proof. If he went to Captain Winters with this, the Net Force agent would recommend Matt for a future career as a mystery novelist. But he wouldn't be able to use Net Force to take on Finch—or the Callivants—without a lot more evidence and a whole lot less conjecture than Matt could currently provide.

What would Monty Newman do in a case like this?

He'd admit he was stumped and hope that Lucullus Marten's big, fat brain would get them out from behind the eight ball, Matt told himself.

Lacking Lucullus Marten—or even Oswald Derbent— there didn't seem much that Matt could do with his suspicions.

That was when the virtmail message came in. It just took over Matt's computer, extinguishing the map of New Jersey and replacing it with a display of floating letters—no posting, no headings:

I know what you're doing. We've got to meet. Buffalo Bridge, 45 minutes.

Even as Matt sat, gawking, the individual letters making up the message began to dissolve. The message turned into a gray smudge, then the display went completely clear.

Matt still sat, staring. Except for the fact that the Jersey map was gone, he could almost believe he'd been having some sort of daydream.

"Computer," he suddenly snapped. "Display my most recent virtmail message."

The item that swam into view was the "Dave Lowen" ancient police report, the time stamp falling during the time Matt had ridden home with Nikki Callivant.

"Not that," Matt said, "the next one."

"No other items received," the computer replied.

"Oh, no?" Matt growled. "Computer, what happened to the New Jersey map projection?"

"That display was terminated," the computer's silver voice reported.

"How?"

"The display was terminated," Matt's computer repeated.

Matt rose from his chair. Great. He didn't have the cryptic message. He didn't even have a record of it. And, of course, he didn't have a clue as to who sent it. Could it be the second hacker in the group of mystery enthusiasts? Could it be Deep Throat?

Whoever sent the message might be all of the above. The thing was, he or she wanted a physical meeting. No hiding behind virtual masks or proxies. The setting was the Buffalo Bridge, a landmark spanning Rock Creek—right on the border of Georgetown. It was within walking distance from Georgetown University, and not all that far from Father Flannery's parish. It was probably one of the simmers—and Matt wanted to talk to them, too. . . .

Matt wrote a note to his parents, explaining that he had some important research to do. Then he slipped on a coat. If he expected to get down to the Buffalo Bridge in time, he'd have to push it—

Dashing out of the house, Matt had reached the sidewalk before he became aware of the man running up behind him. Actually, the guy was hard to ignore. He was puffing like a set of bellows.

And the gun he held was boring into Matt's back, right through his coat.

"Turn. Slowly." Matt didn't know what made it scarier—the one-word commands, or the fact that the gunman was still gasping for breath.

"Walk. It's the open car door."

Matt did as he was commanded, retracing his steps. He couldn't miss his destination. The late-model black car had its door open, throwing a funnel of light into the winter evening darkness.

"Inside."

The pistol stayed in Matt's back all the way down. Then it transferred to his ear as he sank into the plushly upholstered seat. He kept his head still, but his eyes ached as they strained to the left for a glimpse of his kidnapper.

It was an old guy, once athletic, now fat, and red-faced from the brief run from his car to intercept Matt. The man was bald, with iron-gray hair, and looked vaguely familiar. Where had Matt seen him before?

Not him, but a younger version, grinning in a faded flatfilm photograph.

"Clyde Finch," he gasped.

"You don't know when to stop, do you, Junior?" Finch's gun hand stayed rock-solid against Matt's head while his other hand fumbled in his pocket. It came out holding a fistful of clinking metal that Finch tossed into Matt's lap. "Put 'em on."

Matt glanced down. Handcuffs! Stiffly, unwillingly, he again did as he was commanded.

Still holding the gun on Matt, Finch brought his free hand down hard on each of Matt's wrists, squeezing the cuffs tightly so they bit into Matt's flesh.

"Now you'll be less likely to try something stupid." Finch used a foot to push Matt to the far side of the car. He grunted as he joined his prisoner in the back seat.

The snub-nosed pistol that covered Matt was right out of an old detective flick. It had none of the clean lines of the automatics favored by the stars of cop shows and spy movies. No, this was an ugly old Smith & Wesson, a nasty little machine built to create death at close ranges.

"That cannon you're carrying has to be ancient." Matt forced the words out between dry lips.

"More than twice as old as you are," Finch replied. "It was my backup piece when I was on the Haddington force. But don't worry. The ammo is new. And this old fart knows a few new tricks. I sent you that message to see if you were too nosey to live. And you took the bait. Since you recognized me, it's time to take you out."

"Don't be crazy," Matt replied. "You can't shoot me in a car."

"Why not?" the old man demanded. "This sucker has tinted windows, and it's soundproofed better than some places I've lived." He grinned, showing off a set of tobacco-stained teeth. "Besides, cars are always disposable—and replaceable."

"I guess, nowadays, that's not as easy," Matt sniped back—the only thing he could do with his hands cuffed. "Not as easy, say, as ditching a red '65 Corvette in a wildlife sanctuary, and stealing a replacement."

Finch jumped as if he'd been stabbed, his red face going pale. He brought up the pistol. Matt had no doubt where he was about to aim. He stared at the stubby little weapon as it swung toward him.

But Finch's gun arm suddenly twitched back the way it had come. The man's whole body hunched forward, his hand like a claw on the butt of the gun. The pistol went off, its discharge deafening in the small area of the closed car. A bullet tore into the upholstery of the car seat back in front of them.

Recoil sent the snub-nosed pistol flying from Clyde Finch's hand. But he didn't go for the gun. Instead, Finch slumped back in his seat, clutching at his chest, his breath coming in shallow, agonized pants.

17

A heart attack, Matt thought, looking at Clyde Finch's gray, sweaty face. The old man's expression was a mask of terror as Matt reached for him. Finch heaved, and a small trickle of vomit leaked from the side of his mouth. He said something—at least his lips moved—but Matt's ears, still stunned by the noise of the gun going off, couldn't hear.

"Do you have pills?" Matt realized he was shouting, but he couldn't help himself.

Finch nodded, fumbling his coat open. Matt went for tissues to wipe the old man's mouth—and realized he was still handcuffed.

"Where are the keys for these?" Matt shouted.

The gray-faced man was picking feebly at a vest pocket. Matt reached over. His fingers felt like they belonged to someone else, half-starved for blood by the tightly locked cuffs. Finally he brought out an inch-long metal cylinder with a key chain attached.

Matt examined the cylinder. Apparently, it was supposed to open at a twist—some sort of airtight pillbox.

"If I try to open this with my fingers feeling like sausages, we may lose the pills inside," he said, rattling the keys. "Will one of these open the cuffs? You'd better hope they do. . . ."

Finch's waxy lips formed an O as Matt struggled to unlock his cuffs.

Finally finding a small key that seemed to fit the locks on the cuffs, Matt wiggled it around until he had it firmly in the lock, then tried to turn it. He finally succeeded, leaving the cuffs dangling from one wrist while his free hand went for tissues. He managed to get Finch's mouth clean, stretching the sick man full-length on the backseat. As he knelt over him, Matt's knee landed on the snub-nosed pistol still lying on the floor. He kicked it under the front seat while he opened the pillbox, setting one of the tiny tablets inside under the stricken man's tongue.

Matt didn't know what effect the cold outside air would have on Finch, but it couldn't be good for him to be breathing cordite fumes. He opened the door to clear the car interior, dug out his wallet-phone, and punched in 911.

Moments later Matt leaned against the car fender as paramedics trundled Finch into an ambulance. The emergency services people hadn't said anything about the bullet hole in the front seat. Matt had no idea what the ER doctors would make of the empty shoulder holster Finch was wearing.

He tried to kill me, and I end up saving his life, Matt thought, still feeling shell-shocked. He headed up the walkway to his house, his feet moving faster and faster as he neared the door. By the time he got inside, Matt was running. He tore down the hallway to his room, one hand digging for his wallet and the card Nikki Callivant had given him.

Matt almost punched his computer console into life. Reading from the card, he barked out Nikki Callivant's private communications code.

A moment later Nikki's elegant face appeared in the

holographic display. "Matt?" she said in surprise. He could still barely hear her.

"Does your Grandpa Clyde use a short-barreled Smith and Wesson?" he demanded.

"Why are you shouting? What's—"

"I'm shouting because I'm half-deaf! Your dear great-grandfather kidnapped me—tried to use that gun on me. The only reason I'm here is because he had a heart attack."

"You're not making any sense," Nicola Callivant said, but her expression was beginning to get frightened. "Grandpa Clyde—"

She suddenly looked over her shoulder, apparently holding a conversation with someone who'd come into her room. Matt couldn't hear what they were saying. If the pickup was getting it, their voices were too soft for his abused ears to register. But he could imagine the news Nikki was receiving.

Her face was pale when she turned back to Matt. "What did you do to him?"

"It's more what he did to me. Apparently, he was ready to kill if that would protect your family's dirty little secrets."

"You're crazy," she said flatly.

"Fine," Matt spat. "I'll call my connections at Net Force, and let them find Grandpa Clyde's gun. Let him explain what he was doing in that car in front of my house—"

"No!" Nikki cut in. She looked at her watch. "You're at home?"

"Where else?"

"I can be there in forty-five minutes. Will you at least wait that long?"

Matt nodded.

She cut the connection.

Sagging back onto his bed, Matt took in a long breath. Forty-five minutes. It was a bad omen.

He staggered to his computer. This time he wasn't

leaving anything to chance. He was going to leave word for Leif and James Winters, telling them exactly what was going on, in case his plan to get the evidence for who was really responsible for all this mess didn't pan out. One way or another, he was going to put a stop to this.

Nikki Callivant actually beat her estimated time of arrival, but even so, she cut it pretty fine. Matt's parents were almost due back home. Matt had left a message for them, too.

He wanted them to know exactly where he was going.

Swinging round onto the expressway that would take them to Delaware, Nikki was tight-lipped and quiet. Finally she asked, "Are your ears any better?"

"Yeah. The ringing's down to a mild roar. Looks like I didn't bust an eardrum."

"When I was little, Grandpa Clyde sometimes took me to a firing range. He always made sure I wore these big plastic earmuffs. Even so, the noise was awful."

"I'll tell you something. It's even worse in a small space like a car. Maybe because it's so sealed in." As Matt spoke he cracked the window, letting a trickle of cold air play across his face. By this time he should be sitting down for supper with his folks.

He hoped the note he'd left didn't scare them.

"You're treating what—whatever happened like some big conspiracy," Nikki's voice took on an odd note as she flashed him a look from behind the steering wheel. "My family—we're not like that."

"Let's see how your dad and the rest react to your new, lower-class friend," Matt replied.

He suddenly understood her tone. Nikki wasn't trying to convince him. She was trying to convince herself.

They rolled on, barely speaking, through suburbs and then a stretch of country. Matt glanced at his watch as they pulled up at a gated compound. Nikki had actually shaved a few minutes off her previous record.

A guy in a blue coat—obviously a guard—appeared from the gatehouse. He greeted Nikki respectfully, but kept his eyes on Matt.

"It's all right, Marcus," Nikki said. "He's a friend."

The gate opened, and they were in.

Matt supposed he must have seen pictures of the Callivant compound somewhere. In real life the place seemed smaller, less—well, *rich*—than he expected. There was a big house, though, blazing with light. Nikki parked her car, got out, and took Matt's arm.

Matt might have thought that was funny, but he was glad of the silent support as they went up the front steps. As they crossed the entrance hall, a man who was just a little too tight-faced to be handsome intercepted them.

"Nikki, Marcus said you'd just come in. I thought you said you were going to the hos—" The man suddenly realized there was a stranger present and shut up.

"This is my father, Daniel Callivant," Nikki said. "Dad, this is Matt Hunter. He's the one who called the ambulance for Grandpa Clyde. That was pretty nice when you think about it. Matt says Grandpa Clyde was trying to shoot him at the time."

Daniel Callivant handled it pretty well, but he hadn't expected any such confrontation in his own home. For an instant, just an instant, his unguarded expression revealed that he knew who Matt was—and what Clyde Finch had been doing off in Maryland.

Nikki caught it. Her breath sucked in, then she said, "I think we'd better see Grandfather Callivant."

"He's working on a speech," her father objected.

"I think this is more important." Nikki began leading Matt deeper into the house.

"Nikki!" her father called after her.

"There's a solarium in the back," Nikki told Matt as they skirted a formal dining room. "It sort of serves as a community den. We do a lot of living on this level because of the Senator—"

A door stood ajar ahead of them, and the sound of a

national newscast leaked out. Then the door opened all the way, revealing a man in a wheelchair.

"Nikki, what are you doing here when Clyde needs you?"

Walter Callivant still looked like a senator, even though it had been years since he'd held the office. He had a mane of pure white hair, and a handsome, dignified face, with, as one political writer tried to put it poetically, "the look of eagles."

On closer examination, however, the eagle looked old. Callivant's skin stretched tightly over his bones. A blanket covered him from the waist down, concealing legs that hadn't been used almost as long as Matt had been alive.

The Senator's cold blue eyes shifted from Nikki to Matt. From the look of contemptuous dislike, Matt suspected that Daniel Callivant had managed a quick briefing. Maybe a place this big had house phones.

"I have to see Grandfather," Nikki insisted.

"With this—person?" The Senator's tone of voice would have been better suited if he'd said "worm."

The Callivant patriarch rolled his automated wheelchair nearer. "Do you realize what you're doing, Nicola? You're a Callivant. That means you have certain—family responsibilities. Your grandfather is inside, waiting to see the coverage of his announcement that he's seeking the nomination."

He rounded on Matt. "And you bring this—what? This would-be muckraker—*blackmailer* into our house? Do you want to destroy your grandfather's chances of getting back into the Senate?

Anger overcame Matt's sense of intimidation, and he finally found his voice. "Oh, sure," he said. "What are the lives of a few peons versus the chance of having a Callivant back where he belongs?"

"Shut your mouth, you miserable thief!" the Senator thundered nearly as well as Lucullus Marten. "I know your type only too well—and I've dealt with them over the years. You're like the rats in the wall, emerging to nibble, nibble, nibble away at your betters, coming out to spread lies like some loathsome disease. You're a ghoul, digging up the dead past to feed on it!"

It was quite a speech, even if the Senator wound up mixing his metaphors a bit. "So tell me, Senator. Did you send Clyde Finch out for a bit of pest control?"

"You don't seem to realize your position, boy." The Senator's face became downright sinister as he ran his wheelchair almost onto Matt's feet. "You're an intruder in my home."

"There are people who know where I am," Matt replied as steadily as he could. "Lots of them. And I have friends who know exactly what you've been doing. If anything happens to me, Net Force will be asking questions."

"I've deposed directors of the FBI," the elder Callivant sneered. "Do you think you can scare me with some low-level agent in a wash-and-wear suit?"

"I think that I'm here as an invited guest. And if you try anything stupid, you'll discover you're not above the law."

"I think you're the stupid one. I've been arranging the laws as it seems fit to me since before your parents were born. You've got a nerve to lecture me. Not to mention a foolish streak. The truth is what we Callivants say it is. If we say you're an intruder—"

"I invited him," Nikki ground out from between her clenched teeth.

"You are being just as foolish as he is, dear." The Senator aimed a cold look at her. "You're not thinking clearly. Sadly, it's a trait that runs in our female line."

"Don't think you can do to me what you did to Aunt Rosaline," Nikki flared. "With that convenient 'nervous breakdown.' "

Walter Callivant's cold eyes looked at his great-granddaughter as if she were some sort of lab specimen. "Yes," he said, "you're very like Rosaline. But once she'd been committed and started on medication, she became much less of a problem."

A new voice came from the doorway. "That's enough, Father."

Matt remembered Megan's description of the pleasant Walter G. Callivant she'd met at that formal hoedown. But the gray-haired man who faced them now looked more like the harassed junior senator the comedians all made fun of. It was the hunted look in his eyes. "What's this all about, Nikki?" Walter G. asked.

"It's about Priscilla Hadding."

Nikki's grandfather flinched, but he didn't retreat. "It was an accident," he said softly. "But I've never been able to forget it. All these years, it's stuck with me. We— I was just about your age. We'd gone to a party—a pretty rowdy affair. Silly and I—that's what we called her, you know."

He took a deep breath. "Silly and I were out in the Corvette, arguing as usual. Then she was cursing at me, going to leave. I gunned the engine to drown out what she was saying. That Corvette—that was more car than I could handle. Somehow, it got into gear—"

Walter G. Callivant's face was no longer bumbling or vague as he looked back on that memory. "It almost flew down the road. By the time I got it stopped—Silly's foot—it had been caught in the door—"

His eyes squeezed shut, and he brought up his hands to cover his face. "But it was an accident," his muffled voice came from between his fingers.

"A bad-looking accident—especially for a Callivant," Walter Senior suddenly spoke. "He was my son. It would have reflected badly—"

"On *you*," Nikki said angrily. "So you covered it up. Clyde Finch saw his chance. He got hold of a similar car and switched the license plates. It got him a new job, and, thanks to his daughter, he got into the family—sort of."

"At least Marcia knows how to keep her mouth shut!"

Walter Callivant, Sr., didn't look so senatorial all of a sudden.

But Nikki was far from shutting up. "You let Mrs. Hadding dangle all those years to protect your lie. How—"

"Angela Hadding is a typical example of what happens if you let a woman speak her mind," Walter Senior cut in.

I bet that attitude must have gone over well with the women voters, Matt noted silently. Then he spoke. "But freezing out a childless widow wasn't enough. You had to keep people away from those old court records. So you overreacted when your security system sent off hacker alarms. Clyde Finch managed to trace the hacker to the D.C. area. He must have spread his search pretty wide to come up with Ed Saunders's mystery sim."

"I thought he was stretching things, too, when he came up with that scenario," the senator said. "But after our legal people sent the usual letters, we suffered a major hacker attack." He turned to Nikki. "The hacker erased our family history site, filling it with nasty questions about Priscilla Hadding. And he wanted to blackmail us."

Matt stared at him. "And that was enough to justify killing Ed Saunders and Oswald Derbent as well as the hacker?"

The eyes of the man in the wheelchair blazed with fury. Apparently it was the first time in decades that someone had questioned Walter Callivant's decisions. "We didn't know who the hacker was—we only suspected it was somebody in that sim. Saunders's death was an accident," Callivant snapped. "Finch had arranged for him to be mugged. We wanted to get the list of sim participants from him. We figured we could step up the pressure on all of you and find the hacker."

"It certainly stepped up the pressure on Ed," Matt agreed ironically. "It killed him." He shook his head. "And it was totally unnecessary. The poor guy had al-

ready sent your lawyers the letter naming the participants."

"How were we to know?" Callivant Senior demanded.
"The fool tried to run and slipped on the ice."

Matt nodded in understanding. "Of course—it's much
more sensible to stand around and get beaten up."

Callivant was so angry, he wasn't censoring himself at
all. "I said it was an accident. What about you? What
about the threats you sent us after Saunders died? You
claimed you had enough already to destroy my son's candidacy."

"Not me," Matt told him. "The hacker, we suspect, was
Harry Knox. You must have thought so, too, once your
lawyers got Saunders's list. If you checked people's
backgrounds, you'd have come upon the juvenile charges
against Knox for hacking." He leaned forward. "Was the
failure of his truck's brakes supposed to be another warning?"

"We were dealing with a criminal," Callivant said
stiffly. "My grandson Daniel devised a response and saw
the job through."

"Just like a spy novel," Matt continued to needle information out of the old man. "Did Daniel get his hands
dirty monkeying with the brakes, or was it a high-tech
job, like what happened to the autobus? Did he use an
EMP to send the truck's circuits haywire?

"It's a secret technology." A little belatedly Callivant
Senior clamped his lips shut.

"A government secret, you mean," Matt said. "As op-
posed to a Callivant secret. By the way, Net Force is still
looking at that bus. I hope Daniel hid his tracks well."

"But you got the hacker," Nikki burst out. "Matt told
me that Knox had a computer full of information about
us. Why did you continue to go after those people? Why
did Oswald Derbent's house burn down? Why did you
almost kill Matt?"

"You believe him?" Scorn sizzled in the Senator's
voice. "Unauthorized access to files continued—*after* that

Knox person was eliminated. Worse, it took place on an even more sophisticated level. We targeted those who were most likely to use hacking technology. Derbent had been a systems auditor before he devoted himself to book collecting. And the boy"—Callivant jerked his chin at Matt—"he's an obvious danger.

"Unauthorized access," Nikki echoed, looking numb. "That—that was me. I started looking into the files. I heard about all those people getting in trouble because of the old Hadding case, and I wanted to see what it was all about."

"You?" Senator Callivant looked as if he were on the verge of having a stroke. *"You?"*

"I got one person killed," Nikki went on, her voice hollow. "And three more almost killed."

"You didn't do a thing," Matt said grimly. "Your father did, though. I bet he had a hand in the 'accident' at Derbent's. And the Senator already admitted the use of your father's spy-toy on the bus."

Callivant Senior was still concentrating on Nikki's treachery. "You are no longer part of this family," he grated. "You Judas!"

"I wish *I* weren't a part of this family!"

Everyone had forgotten about Walter G. Now they turned to him. Nikki's grandfather suddenly looked years older than he had mere minutes before. "Father, what I did was an accident. But you, Clyde . . . Daniel . . . you killed—"

"We protected you." Years of frustration and disappointment sounded in the Senator's voice. "We knew you needed protection."

"Just what I needed, Father," Walter G. said bitterly. "More blood on my hands. I feel so . . . safe."

He stepped around his father's wheelchair and strode quickly away.

"Walter!" the Senator called after him. "Son!"

He turned a glare on Matt that should have incinerated him. "Weakling," Callivant muttered.

For a long moment the Senator sat in stormy silence, thinking. Then he stabbed a finger down on the armrest of his wheelchair. "Daniel? You heard it all?"

"Yes, sir," Daniel Callivant's voice came through a speaker hidden somewhere in the chair's circuitry.

"He'll be no use to us," the old man's voice thickened. "Again. We'll have to—take care of the situation." Matt didn't like the look Callivant suddenly turned on him. "I think the intruder scenario—"

"Marcus saw him come in with my daughter," Daniel Callivant interrupted over the speaker.

"Can't you handle him?" the Senator demanded impatiently.

"And create another Clyde Finch?" Daniel asked. Walter Callivant's hands turned into clawlike fists on the armrests. "Come here!"

A moment or two later Daniel Callivant appeared in the hallway behind Matt and Nikki. "Grandfather."

"I've thought it through," the Senator said. "Nikki unwisely brought this boy home. He attacked her, and while we tried to subdue—"

"No!" Nikki screamed the word. "I won't—"

"Of course, she had to be sedated," Walter Callivant's voice remorselessly rolled along. He glared at his son. "The alternative, of course, is that the young animal killed her."

Daniel Callivant went pale, looking at his daughter. "No. Grandfather—"

"You heard how she betrayed us. She'll betray us all. Choose, Daniel. The family, or this little—"

"Grandfather! Please!"

"You're a Callivant! You have no choice!"

"I-I can't—"

"You expect me to?" Walter Senior smashed a hand down on his withered legs. "I tell you again, Daniel. You have no choice."

Daniel Callivant's tightly wrapped facade was gone. His lips trembled as he looked at his daughter.

Nikki's eyes went back and forth between the family patriarch and her father, the horror in them growing.

Matt began to prepare himself for a hopeless leap. If Daniel was armed, he was probably dead already. But he had to fight!

Daniel Callivant opened his mouth to answer.

But he was cut off by a harsh blatting sound from the speaker in Walter Senior's chair. He pushed a button, and a different voice came out of the speaker.

"Sir! The police are here—they say there's an intruder!"

18

A wild look passed between Walter and Daniel Callivant. But Nikki spoke first.

"Let them in, Marcus!"

The noise Walter Callivant made would have been more appropriate coming from an animal. "Marcus!" he shouted when he got control of himself.

But Nikki was already on her knees, tearing something loose from the wheelchair. Wordlessly she held up the transceiver speaker.

"You—!" The Senator sent his chair into a wild pivot, knocking Nikki to the floor.

Matt leaped forward, grabbing both of Walter Callivant's wrists, keeping them from the wheelchair controls. "Try that again—" he threatened.

Behind him, he heard the door slam open and heavy footsteps coming their way.

Daniel Callivant stepped aside.

Walter Callivant wrenched himself loose, turning to the excited-looking young police officer who accompanied Marcus the gate guard.

"The intruder—" the Senator began.

"We're after him!" the cop exclaimed. "He came barreling out in a car the second the gate opened! My partner's in pursuit. I'm here to preserve the scene until the investigators come."

His voice began to wind down as he looked around at the tableau in front of him. "Everything all right here?"

Nikki Callivant got up from the floor. "My great-grandfather had an accident," she said. "My friend Matt went to help him."

"But who drove out?" Walter Callivant suddenly sounded like the stereotype of the confused old man. He suddenly looked up at Daniel. "Walter!"

He means Walter G., Matt realized.

"My son," the Senator clarified. "He's been under some strain preparing his candidacy. Perhaps—ah, perhaps a mistake was made—"

Matt watched the man fumble desperately, trying to construct a story.

Walter G. called the cops and made sure that they would chase him. The question is, where does he intend to lead them?

"You'd better contact your superiors," Daniel Callivant spoke up. "Tell them my father is in the car they're after."

It was neither a high-speed pursuit nor one of those notorious slow-speed chases. Walter G. Callivant left Haddington driving exactly at the speed limit. Local cops were joined by Delaware State Police, and then by Maryland troopers.

And, of course, a fleet of news choppers circled overhead. Matt, Nikki, and the other Callivants were able to follow developments on HoloNews.

The house was filled with various police representatives, legal advisers, and P.R. people. Somewhere along the line, Captain Winters showed up.

"Your parents got in touch with me," he said. "And I

got that delayed message you left. You might want to know that I've dispatched agents to keep an eye on Finch until he's fit to take into custody. I assume you'll be pressing charges? Then I scrambled a chopper—just in case it might be advisable to come by."

He was talking with colleagues when the chase came to its climax. Walter G. Callivant drove his car through the gates of the Cowper's Bluff Nature Preserve. He took an old path directly to the bluff and drove his car over the precipice and into the Chesapeake below.

"That's where they must have hidden his real car," Matt whispered to the weeping Nikki.

"And why they put it off-limits all these years," she choked back.

"I'm very sorry for your loss," Captain Winters told Daniel Callivant.

"My father must have been under more of a strain than we thought." Nikki's dad looked desperate to get out of the room. Maybe he was afraid there was a suicide note with dangerous confessions upstairs.

Winters maintained his grip on the man's hand for an extra second, giving him an appraising look.

Sure, Matt thought. *He's got to be checking him out over that EMP gizmo.*

Winters turned to Matt. "Can I give you a lift home?"

"I'll drive him home." Nikki Callivant wiped the tears from her delicate cheeks. "And I won't be back, Father. Mom has some relatives in Washington. I'll arrange to stay with them."

She took a deep breath. "Remember how we were discussing whether I'd take my senior year abroad? I'm going. And when I come back, I'll be of age to use the trust fund Uncle George left me. It's not Callivant money."

Nikki paused. "But then, I'm not a Callivant anymore."

Daniel Callivant stared, stricken, as his daughter began leading Matt to the door. "Nikki! You can't be serious! We have to talk—"

She looked over her shoulder. "Not now," Nikki said. "Not ever."

Captain Winters walked with them, sending a puzzled, suspicious glance Matt's way. But if Nikki wasn't going to say anything, neither was Matt.

He didn't know if the truth behind Walter G. Callivant's suicide would ever come out. He couldn't even be sure the Senator and Daniel would receive just punishment. A lot of things happened behind the scenes in Washington—especially when national security was involved. He knew he and Winters would do their best to put those responsible for the sim deaths behind bars, but it wasn't exactly a certainty that these powerful men would get what was coming to them. That all lay in the future.

Right now Matt wanted to get home. But before he did that, he had to make sure Nikki Callivant got safely to her car and away from the men who had almost killed her to further their own ambitions—her family.

Matt remembered an ending line from an old Lucullus Marten story—something that was pure Monty Newman.

Maybe what I did was more personal than professional. But when a girl has just disowned her family, she could use an arm around her shoulders.

That's exactly what Matt gave her.

VIRTUAL CRIME. REAL PUNISHMENT.

TOM CLANCY'S NET FORCE®

Created by Tom Clancy and Steve Pieczenik
written by Bill McCay

The Net Force fights all criminal activity online. But a group of teen experts
knows just as much about computers as their adult superiors.

They are the Net Force Explorers...

❑ **VIRTUAL VANDALS**	0-425-16173-0/$4.99
❑ **THE DEADLIEST GAME**	0-425-16174-9/$4.99
❑ **ONE IS THE LONELIEST NUMBER**	
	0-425-16417-9/$4.99
❑ **THE ULTIMATE ESCAPE**	0-425-16939-1/$4.99
❑ **THE GREAT RACE**	0-425-16991-X/$4.99
❑ **END GAME**	0-425-17113-2/$4.99
❑ **CYBERSPY**	0-425-17191-4/$4.99
❑ **SHADOW OF HONOR**	0-425-17303-8/$4.99

Prices slightly higher in Canada

Payable by Visa, MC or AMEX only ($10.00 min.), No cash, checks or COD. Shipping & handling:
US/Can. $2.75 for one book, $1.00 for each add'l book; Int'l $5.00 for one book, $1.00 for each
add'l. Call (800) 788-6262 or (201) 933-9292, fax (201) 896-8569 or mail your orders to:

Penguin Putnam Inc. P.O. Box 12289, Dept. B Newark, NJ 07101-5289 Please allow 4-6 weeks for delivery. Foreign and Canadian delivery 6-8 weeks.	Bill my: ❑ Visa ❑ MasterCard ❑ Amex _____ (expires) Card# _____ Signature _____

Bill to:

Name _____

Address _____City _____

State/ZIP _____Daytime Phone # _____

Ship to:

Name _____	Book Total	$	_____
Address _____	Applicable Sales Tax	$	_____
City _____	Postage & Handling	$	_____
State/ZIP _____	Total Amount Due	$	_____

This offer subject to change without notice.   Ad # 821 (6/00)

Penguin Putnam Inc.
Online

Your Internet gateway to a virtual environment with hundreds of entertaining and enlightening books from Penguin Putnam Inc.

While you're there, get the latest buzz on the best authors and books around—

Tom Clancy, Patricia Cornwell, W.E.B. Griffin, Nora Roberts, William Gibson, Robin Cook, Brian Jacques, Catherine Coulter, Stephen King, Jacquelyn Mitchard, and many more!

Penguin Putnam Online is located at http://www.penguinputnam.com

PENGUIN PUTNAM NEWS

Every month you'll get an inside look at our upcoming books and new features on our site. This is an ongoing effort to provide you with the most up-to-date information about our books and authors.

Subscribe to Penguin Putnam News at http://www.penguinputnam.com/ClubPPI